PROWL

SPECIAL EDITION

SPLICED LOVE SERIES
BOOK 1

NATALIE STARKOSS

For those longing for acceptance and fearing they'll never find it.

Prowl's bite is for you.

CONTENTS

HEADS UP!

As an Australian Author, I write using Australian (British) spelling & punctuation, NOT American.

This means my American friends will notice a few differences when reading my books: Mom is Mum, color is colour, recognize is recognise etc. (We play differently with the letters O, U, S & Z and tend to add extra L's)

These aren't spelling mistakes, just our way of doing things down under.

Happy Reading!

Nat xx

TRIGGER WARNINGS

This book contains content that may be upsetting for some readers. For a full list of potential triggers, please visit my website and check my trigger warning page.

If you think something should be added to the current list, please email me directly.

Your mental health is important.

Please take good care of it.

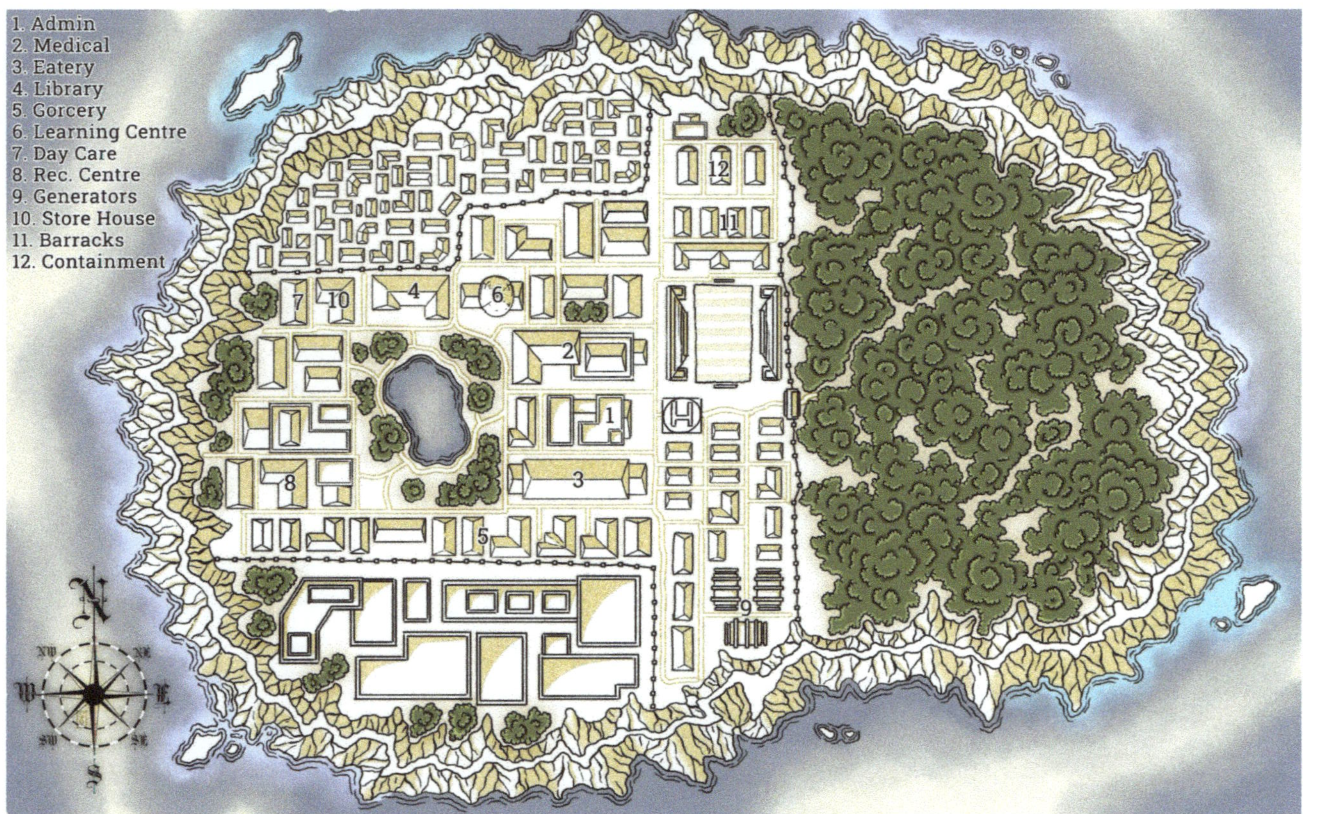

1. Admin
2. Medical
3. Eatery
4. Library
5. Gorcery
6. Learning Centre
7. Day Care
8. Rec. Centre
9. Generators
10. Store House
11. Barracks
12. Containment

CHAPTER 1
DAFF

The metal death trap dipped, and I closed my eyes, swallowing against the bile in the back of my throat.

They hadn't told us how we'd be travelling, other than a date and time. Like everything else about this job, the details had been kept on a need-to-know basis.

Apparently, I didn't need to know much.

Mandy's hand in mine gripped tighter, the tips of her nails digging into my skin.

A reminder I wasn't the only one terrified.

Static blasted through my headphones, and a voice punched through the noise, keeping time with the soldier's lips, strapped in at the front of the helicopter.

"We're sixty seconds out from landing. Remain seated until you're released from your harness and directed to exit."

I gave Mandy's hand a squeeze then slipped from her grip, the both of us wrapping our fingers around the thick straps holding us in.

My stomach floated for a few terrifying seconds, then a soft bump signalled solid ground. Smooth. Easy. Just like they promised.

I pressed my hand to my chest, hoping the pressure would convince my pounding heart we weren't still on the brink of exploding into scattered body parts, too melted to identify.

Two soldiers jumped into action, working on releasing our restraints while another directed us off single file, pointing towards a shuttle bus.

We ran towards it, our heads ducked against the wind slamming into us from the rotating blades. I took a window seat halfway down the shuttle and Mandy slipped in beside me, rubbing her hands down her thighs as her eyes darted between windows.

It looked like we'd landed in the belly of a dead volcano, fully reclaimed by nature before being disturbed by the military.

Lush green slopes rose to form sheer cliffs around us. On our right, nature ran wild, the enormous trees walled off by an insanely tall, chain-link fence topped with three rounds of razor wire. Our left was packed with cookie-cutter rows of buildings, their roofs lined with solar panels.

"Oh my god," Mandy whispered, "Where are we?"

The shuttle door slammed, making us all jump.

"Eyes on me, ladies!"

The soldier stood at the front of our bus, legs spread, shoulders rigid, hands clasped behind his back. He wore the same fatigues as those on our helicopter, but he had two guns strapped to his waist, one a lot chunkier than the other.

"I understand it's been a long trip, and you're tired. You'll be able to stretch your legs in just a few more minutes."

"Where are we?" The woman sitting behind us asked. She had pale skin spattered with freckles, making the dark circles under her eyes stand out. I was pretty sure she'd introduced herself as Andi.

"We call this base The Compound. It's your new home for the next two years."

Questions exploded around me.

"Yeah, but where are we?"

"We crossed a lot of water."

"Is it Hawaii?"

"Not many other islands are this green."

He held up his hand, stopping the verbal avalanche.

"We have a duty to ensure the health and safety of every person on base. For a number of our residents, their location, therefore this base, is classified. I understand the lack of information is frustrating, but it's absolutely necessary."

Another uncomfortable reminder that us plain Janes were walking into this blind.

I'd seen the ad a year ago, offering an obscene amount of money for female applicants twenty-five and over. Either not enough were interested, or they were smart enough to nope out before signing their contracts NDA, because the second time it flagged my attention, the application age had dropped to twenty-one.

The only other requirement? Cutting contact with the rest of the world for two whole years. While others would rather die at the thought, leaving my two jobs and the top bunk in Dad's trailer behind wasn't a big deal. I didn't have any pets. No besties or boyfriends. There was nothing to miss or make me hesitate in signing up besides Dad, who'd pushed me to go.

Because two years was nothing when it meant coming out the other end, able to buy my own home and study anything I wanted with no debt to my name.

Or Dads.

It was a life most people could only dream of, and it was going to be mine.

The shuttle hummed to life, following the single road towards the populated side. It stopped outside a two-story building with admin scrawled across the side in giant block letters.

I leant forward far enough to roll my shoulders without bumping Mandy, trying to ease some of their tension. The brief transfer hadn't been nearly enough time on my feet, not after a full day of travel.

"I wonder why they put the base here? I mean, it's beautiful, but..."

There was no other physical way on or off the island besides the helicopter we'd arrived on. What if there was an emergency and the whole base needed to evacuate?

Mandy shrugged, crowding my personal space again as she looked out my window. "You won't hear any complaints from me. It's gorgeous."

"What do we do when we're bored? There's nowhere to go!"

I nudged Mandy until she moved back, then looked over my shoulder at Tess, the brunette who'd been strapped in across from me during our flight.

"Boring is great. Better than great. Think of all the reading time."

As eclectic as our backgrounds were, the first thing we'd discovered during our awkward introductions was our shared love of reading. And as classified as most of the details were, we'd been promised access to a library that could acquire any reading materials we requested.

Including smut.

Though the officer who'd assured us of it didn't look like he knew what it was.

A few of us had snickered at that, making the poor guy look uncomfortable.

The side door opened, and another military guy stepped

in. He wasn't in uniform, but there was no mistaking the way he moved.

"Welcome to The Compound. My name's Jean and my job is your safety. If you ever have concerns for yourself or a friend, issues you feel aren't being addressed, or feel physically unsafe, you come to me. This," he said, pointing to the building we'd parked in front of, "is Admin. All our main offices are here, including security.

"Lara is my counterpart, and she's waiting for us in conference room two. She'll brief you on why you're here and what you'll spend the next two years doing with us. Follow me."

We hustled off the shuttle and through a set of glass doors. A single hall ran in both directions, filled with glass windows and steel doors. Conference room two had a small keypad beside its door, its solid wall missing the blind covered window the others all had. Inside, two fans lazily spun on the ceiling, its thin, industrial carpet hidden by a huge ass table all twelve of us could fit around.

Jean remained by the door, waiting until we'd all taken our seats before closing it and nodding to the woman standing at the front of the room.

A slender blonde I assumed was Lara.

She greeted us with a tired smile. "Let me start by saying that although I don't yet know you all, I'm honoured to be working with you. You've been through an intense vetting process and have committed to giving up a chunk of your life with very little information. I can wholeheartedly assure you that your sacrifice is for a very good cause."

"And the pay," someone muttered.

Lara's smile dipped a fraction. "It doesn't change the fact that you're here, and your presence will impact many lives for the better."

A message tone sounded, and Lara glanced at Jean,

who'd unclipped his pager. He scanned it then looked up, shaking his head.

She turned her attention back to us.

"Two years ago, an intelligence mission resulted in the discovery of a multifaceted research facility intent on creating a superior breed of soldiers. This included DNA splicing between humans and animals, and a lifetime of tests and experiments on the hybrids they created."

Lara picked up a remote and the wall behind her lit up with pictures. Pictures of prison cells and the creatures inside them. Some had fur. Eyes that reflected the light. Faces with noses and jaws too wide and warped to be human.

"Oh god," someone whispered, echoing my thoughts. "This can't be real."

I pressed a hand to my stomach, churning inside me. "Did you rescue them?"

Lara's gaze found mine. "As many as we could."

She clicked through the next few slides, maintaining a steady pace. "The initial loss of life was staggering. Since then, we've learnt what each hybrid species needs, not just to survive, but to thrive. This compound was created in response to those needs.

"Medical facilities, individual housing, education, trade and work opportunities, and a number of recreational facilities. As a result, this past year has seen our resident hybrids progressing from strength to strength."

She turned off the projector, and Jean flicked the lights back on.

"The likelihood of the outside world accepting them without major fallout is minimal but not impossible. Either way, the hybrids are ready for, and in need of a broader community. Which is where you come in."

A few of us shifted in our seats, but none of us said

anything. I think, like me, they were still in a state of shock. If Lara's words hadn't been enough, the pictures she'd shown us had well and truly shoved us over the line.

"Jean, I'll pass this next part to you. I need to make a call."

Jean nodded as Lara hustled from the room, clutching her pager.

"The hybrid's residential area is restricted, as is yours. All other areas of The Compound, excluding the Wild Zone, are considered shared areas. The hybrids have three designations. Low, Gen and High.

"Low have the same rules and curfews as the rest of The Compound. They have a mixed schedule of work and volunteer hours in their chosen fields, and are free to come and go from all shared areas.

"Gen's curfew ends an hour earlier. They're still participating in at least one mandatory class and are restricted from one or more of the shared areas.

"Hybrids with a High designation aren't allowed in shared areas. Most of these hybrids have chosen to permanently reside in the Wild Zone, on the opposite side of the island. These beings are either unable or unwilling to control their non-human instincts, and often display aggressive or territorial behaviour.

"The Hybrid's you'll be interacting with are all Low and Gen designated. Their experience with females has been minimal until recently. The first were medical personnel, followed by guards, and as of three months ago, Group A, our first round of applicants. You are group B."

Tessa's hand shot up. "Are you saying all the animal people are males?"

Jean raised an eyebrow. "They're called hybrids, or beings. I don't want to hear them referred to by any other name or combination again. It's disrespectful. And yes, all the adults are males. Their ages range from seventeen to twenty-six. The females on base are between four and six years old."

"Why are they so different in age and gender?"

Jean grimaced. "Infants and the younger males were euthanised before we could reach them, and we don't know why there aren't any older females. We're hoping it's because they were focused on developing males first and not because they were kept in another facility."

"Oh god," Mandy whispered.

"I know this is a lot to take in. We'll spend the next few days learning about the different hybrid species living here, safety protocols, things you should watch for, and the way we'd like you to handle your interactions with them. We won't let—"

Lara burst back through the door. "Jean, we've got an issue with Prowl."

"King—"

"Is at his limit."

"We can't—"

"Ladies," she said, turning her back to Jean as she cut him off. "It doesn't happen often, but when shit hits the fan here, it hits hard."

"Lara—"

She paused long enough to glare at him. "They're here to help. Let them help."

Both their pagers went off.

"Shit," Jean muttered, glancing at his before shoving it back on his belt. "I'll get the bus ready and call ahead."

Lara nodded and turned back to us, making eye contact with each one of us.

"Prowl is one of only three lion hybrids left. He's extremely intelligent but ruled by pheromones. If any male other than his brother, King, is close, he attacks his enclosure, causing himself physical harm. Initially, we had two female guards he tolerated, but they left a month ago due to their contract's end.

"King is now the only one Prowl calms for, but King's struggling with his own issues and can't stay for long periods of time. This has resulted in a steady decline for Prowl, who's slowly beating himself to death against his own walls."

"Why can't you leave him on his own?"

"Or sedate him?"

She raised her hand, silencing our questions. "His altered genetics doesn't allow us to sedate him for long. Not safely. And being alone results in the same reaction. We're not sure if it's because of his lion's instinctual need to keep those he identifies as family close, or PTSD, from the life he lived before he was rescued."

"What do you need from us?" I asked, glancing at the others.

"I need you to prepare yourselves. We're going to Prowl's containment area, where I'll be sending you in one at a time, just long enough for Prowl to scent you and react. He'll either settle enough to stop self-harming, or continue to self-destruct."

"What if he doesn't respond to anyone?" Mandy asked, voicing what we all wondered.

Lara's shoulders rose and fell in a hopeless gesture. "Then he'll be dead by the end of the week."

CHAPTER 2
DAFF

Our shuttle drove in silence.

We were still wavering between shocked and horrified. Throw in the spur-of-the-moment trip to spend some alone time with one of them losing their mind and slowly killing himself?

I was freaking terrified.

And nurturing a spark of anticipation.

Because Lara was right.

The hybrids deserved to be protected. They deserved a normal life, or as close to normal as possible. And this hybrid, he deserved more time.

Nothing I'd done had ever mattered before, not like this. I could keel over tomorrow and the only difference I'd have made in the world would be the dent in Dad's medical bills.

I straightened my shoulders, determination strengthening my resolve. If I couldn't help this hybrid, I'd focus on the others. Either way, for the next two years, I was all in.

We passed another electric fence topped with razor wire and stopped outside a long, windowless building. Jean held the outer door open, counting heads as we entered a small waiting room with two chairs and an armed guard. A large, blacked out window filled the wall to his left, a single steel door to his right.

Lara moved to the window, drawing our attention. "This is Prowl's containment area. When I release this door, a lion hybrid named King will pass us. Once he's exited the building, I'll send you in one at a time, closing the door behind you to mute our scents.

"One minute is all we'll need to gauge Prowl's response to you. Our goal is to find someone whose pheromones can penetrate his current state, enough to calm him."

Lara paused, her eyes flicking to Jean. "I won't sugarcoat this. Prowl's in a bad state, mentally and physically, and the sounds he makes are distressing."

She hit a switch on the panel beside her, and the dark window cleared, revealing two identical rooms divided in half by a clear wall streaked with blood.

The male closest to us was huge. Well over six feet tall with wide, heavily muscled shoulders and a long, blonde braid hanging down his back. He turned towards us, as if he'd heard the flick of the switch.

Gasps filled the room.

His face was broader than it should've been, his deep set, liquid gold eyes clearly feline, the black slashes of his pupils stretching the full length between his eyelashes. His nose was flat and wide, his jaw sharp and a touch too long, his thin lips an odd shade of brown.

"That's King." Lara pressed another button. "King, we're here. Could you please step outside while we check Prowl's response to the women? I need you to stay close in case we fail. I don't want him left alone in a heightened state."

His chin fell, looking like he held the weight of the world on his shoulders before nodding.

"Ladies, please step back."

We pressed ourselves against the wall, watching as Lara nodded and the guard pressed his thumb to a scanner beside the door. An alert sounded, then the door thunked and slid open, revealing King and a few seconds of unholy noise that raised goosebumps on my skin.

Up close, King was even bigger than I'd thought.

Loud inhales followed him, but he didn't look at us. He kept his face forward and eyes down, passing us as if we didn't exist.

Did he not want us here? Or did he not have the best social skills?

"Prowl's behind an eight-inch, bullet-proof wall, and while his door has bars, there's no physical way he can get through them. Do your best to stay calm. He can't reach or harm you, as long as you keep your distance from his door."

Deep breaths and shuffling feet answered her.

"If we can't calm Prowl long enough for him to eat and heal, he will die. After a lifetime of torture, experiments and abuse, you have a chance at easing him. Of saving his life. You could be his miracle. All you need to do is stand there."

As scared as I was, they'd made it clear I was safe. And if all I needed to do was stand there, to know if it was me he needed?

I could absolutely do that.

As for being stuck in there with him for the next two years?

I'd deal with it when and if it happened.

I dropped my arms from around my waist and stood a little taller. Beside me, Mandy and a few others lifted their chins.

"Ready?" Lara asked.

An alert sounded, and the door opened, releasing the noise trapped within.

My gut clenched, fighting between compassion and

terror. It was almost a roar, but guttural, and still hauntingly human.

How could a single voice express such rage and pain at the same time?

Tessa was first, and a quick head count told me I was fourth in line. She exited with tears running down her cheeks and Lara shaking her head at Jean.

Number two came out hiccuping.

Number three was pale, fists clenched by her sides.

"Next," Lara said, making eye contact with me.

Mandy, who'd had her head on my shoulder, jolted as I stepped forward.

The door slid closed behind me, a wall of metal trapping us together. His roar turned wild, his body slamming the clear wall, leaving behind a fresh smear of blood.

He was just as big as King, but his hair was wild, and the thick beard covering his face couldn't quite hide his hollowed cheeks or the dark skin beneath his eyes. Bruises covered his torso like a Gothic rainbow, the countless layers of purple and black fading in and out over his body, the worst of it on his shoulders and ribs.

Another wailed roar, followed by another body slam.

Prowl was huge and wild and hurting. My heart ached for him, more than it feared him.

It was crazy to think I could help him. There was nothing different between me and the other women out there. Yet I couldn't deny that something about him called to me, a silent tether, tugging me in his direction.

He threw himself at the wall again, his voice echoing a mix of pain and despair.

"Don't! Please don't."

He froze, his golden eyes finding mine.

"My name's Daff," I whispered, taking a tiny step forward. "People think it's short for Daphne, but it's not.

My mum had a breakdown when she realised she was pregnant again. So she named me Daffodil. She said taking care of a flower was less scary than another child."

I knew I was rambling, telling him things I never shared with anyone, but I didn't know what else to say, and he seemed to be listening.

He lifted his chin, his wide nose scenting the air. His eyes widened, and he lunged forward, but instead of slamming against the wall, it was against the bars of his door, forcing himself flush against them, trying to get as close to me as possible.

Panic sparked, but I ignored it.

"Please."

I shivered as the roughness of his voice ran over every inch of my skin.

"Please, what?"

"Keep talking. Please." He inhaled again, his eyes fluttering closed as he pulled my scent into his lungs.

"Right. I can do that." I huffed out a nervous laugh. "I either word vomit or go silent when I'm nervous, and since you need me to talk... prepare yourself."

A low, smooth rumble filled the room, the sound not quite loud enough to hide his deep, steady breaths.

I guess that meant I was helping?

"Before I took this contract, I was working two jobs and still living at home. Home being a two-bedroom trailer we call Chad. One of my brothers named it when he was little. I don't know why, but the name stuck and it's been Chad ever since."

The alert sounded.

"He's quiet," Jean said, appearing in the doorway next to Lara. Lara's eyes were glued to Prowl, Jean's were on me.

Prowl's lips peeled back, the low rumble replaced by a

deeper, warning sound that raised the hairs on the back of my neck.

"It's okay, Prowl. I'm not taking her away."

His feline eyes flew to mine.

Did he want me to keep talking? Or was he asking me if it was true?

"I'm staying, I think? If that's what you need?"

"Prowl?" Lara asked, stepping towards us.

Jean stayed in the doorway.

Prowl inhaled again, his eyelashes fluttering like they wanted to close, but he was forcing them to stay open—not wanting to take his eyes off me.

"She stays."

Lara nodded. "Okay. Jean, have Anita help you with the rest of group B's intake, and tell King the good news, and that he's free to go."

She looked at me. "What's your name, honey?"

"Daff."

"I'll need Daphne's luggage brought here—"

Prowl's growl stopped her. "It's Daff."

Lara's eyebrows jumped. "My apologies, Daff." Her eyes swung to Jean. "Have Daff's luggage sent here and let the kitchen know to redirect her meals."

"Done. Anything else?"

Lara shook her head. "That's it for now."

Jean gave me a nod, stepped back and closed the door, locking the three of us in.

She pulled out one of the two chairs at the small dining table. "Have a seat."

I glanced at Prowl before I took the offered seat. He still had his forehead pressed against the bars of his door, his eyes tracking my every move.

Lara's fingertips thrummed the table like rain drops. She pressed her lips together, then nodded.

"As I mentioned earlier, Prowl is a lion hybrid. They were the smallest in number, and suffered the highest in losses after their rescue. Now, there are only three of them left. Initially, Prowl did great. He was on par with King, the two of them making incredible progress in every aspect.

"Nine months ago he stopped thriving. He reported sleeping issues, loss of appetite and became increasingly reactive to scents. Males in particular, whether human or hybrid."

"Is that why he's here?"

"While he could maintain control in King's presence, Prowl felt he was holding his brothers progress and recovery back. Solitary was the ideal, since scents would be fewer, and he'd be unable to harm anyone when triggered.

"But the solitude exacerbated his PTSD, which results in him doing everything he can to knock himself out, in order to escape his flashbacks."

Jesus.

"So you came up with this?"

It was a basic one-room, open-plan apartment, mirrored on both sides of Prowl's clear wall. Its only nod to privacy was the floor-length curtain hanging from a track on the roof, that could be pulled across when using the shower or toilet.

"This space allows someone he tolerates to stay with him while keeping them both safe, especially when there's no choice but to leave him on his own. With the two other women gone and King unable to stay more than a few hours per visit, it's happening more than he can tolerate."

"What about you? He seems fine with you being here."

"Prowl has an extremely strong instinctual response to pheromones. For him, King is family. His presence, or rather his pheromones, act like an anchor for Prowl, keeping him present and steady.

"He's responding to your pheromones the same way, and because of it, can maintain a better grasp on his mental clarity and self-control. That's why he's content, and tolerating others."

I looked at Prowl, feeling a tug behind my ribs, pulling in his direction. "What happens now?"

"You'll stay here, with Prowl. We'll make sure you have everything you need, and he'll either start improving, since he'll be able to eat and sleep again, or this calm will fade and we'll lose him for good."

She looked at Prowl. "And I can't bear the thought of losing any more of you. Of you finally gaining your freedom, only to die in another prison."

Lara's eyes swung back to me. "Because this is a prison for him. It might be a whole hell of a lot nicer then his last one, but he's still trapped in there."

The truth of it had my stomach twisting.

"I won't let that happen to you, Prowl. Not if I can help it."

His chin lowered, his thick knuckles turning white as they clenched around the bars of his door.

The buzzer sounded, startling a squeak out of me. Lara stood as the door slid open, revealing a guard with my two suitcases.

Prowl bared his teeth, his growl filling the room.

"It's okay, big guy. I'm staying. They're just dropping off my stuff."

His lips twitched, but the noise stopped, which I took as a major win.

"Someone will bring you your meals, but there are extra snacks under the bench." Lara pointed to a red button beneath a clear square case. "This is for emergencies, both safety and medical. The med team checks in at 7 a.m. most mornings. If you need anything before then, use the phone on the wall. It's a direct line to medical, who can forward your call to whoever you need."

She leant towards me, her expression earnest. "I promise you, you're safe here. Prowl can't get out, and he can't hurt you. Not unless you're intentionally within his reach."

Prowl's growl thundered around us, making Lara flinch, and the guard fly back into our room.

"I won't hurt her." His voice was low, dark, and so damn sure for someone who'd been slowly losing himself for months.

The crazy thing was, I believed him.

"I know," I said, making sure he heard the truth in my words.

He closed his eyes and inhaled again.

"I have things to see to, and Prowl will be calmer if it's just you here. Do you need anything else before I go?"

"I'm good."

"Use the phone if you need someone."

"I will."

"Thank you, Daff," Lara said, her voice softening. "And Prowl? I really hope this sticks for you."

Her voice carried a thread of warmth, like she genuinely cared about him.

It made the heaviness I felt in my chest over the hybrids existence and what they'd been through sit a little lighter.

The door slid shut behind her, the sound of the engaging lock smacking me back into reality.

I licked my dry lips as I met Prowl's steady, feline gaze.

What the hell did I do now?

CHAPTER 3
PROWL

We'd seen pictures.

Watched movies.

Studied the snippets of porn we had access to like our lives depended on it.

None of it had prepared me for the reality of her, for the ache in my hands to touch her, to see if her curves felt firm or soft beneath them, to pull her close and inhale her scent until it stained my soul and never left.

Faded jeans painted her thighs, a rumpled shirt matching the worn look around her eyes. Eyes dark brown and filled with genuine concern, aimed in my direction.

For me. A hybrid.

She was too damn sweet to be near the likes of me.

I'd never felt this close to peace in my life, not even the first morning after our rescue when reality hit, and I knew my brothers and I were free.

If a controlled environment that still had a separate set of laws depending if you were human or hybrid could be called freedom.

Still. It was more than we'd ever hoped for.

Her forehead wrinkled, her pale skin pulling into delicate lines and valleys as she looked around the room.

My chest hurt with the need to comfort her, to return the glimpse of peace she'd given me, just from entering my space.

The ache caught fire, turning into auditory vibrations. I pressed my palm against it, trying to steady it with pressure. It was a strange sensation, a pulsing wave that started in my diaphragm and rolled outwards, filling my chest until it escaped as sound, reaching for her.

I couldn't seem to stop it. And yet, when I thought about it, I didn't want to, despite its strangeness.

Instinct wouldn't let me.

It was telling me that if I couldn't touch her, I needed to do this.

She turned back to me, eyebrows raised, studying me like I had her.

I knew I looked different. As a hybrid, our origin species separated us from each other as much in looks as it did in instincts. Compared to humans? Our differences were staggering.

"Are you purring?"

My palm pushed harder for a moment before wrapping around one of the bars between us.

"Yes?"

Her worry lines deepened. "You don't know?"

"I've never done it before."

Her pink lips, another difference between us, popped open.

"Because of me?"

I nodded, feeling more sure of it. "Felines purr when they're content." The cubs use to do it, whenever King and I visited them. I hadn't considered the possibility that I could too. "And to comfort."

"You're trying to comfort me?"

"You look worried."

Her lips rolled inwards as she looked around the room again. Small couch, large bed, sink and bench in one corner, toilet and shower in the other. It would have mirrored mine, except she had things I didn't. A table and two chairs. Kettle. Breakable dishes in her cupboard.

Things I couldn't be trusted not to harm myself with, when the pull into madness, the crushing loneliness, consumed me and I'd do anything to escape it.

"Overwhelmed is a better word. This place, you... today feels a little unbelievable."

"I'll never hurt you."

Her eyes met mine. "I know."

Did she though? Because I meant it. I already knew I'd protect her with my life.

She crossed the few steps to the couch and flopped onto it, her head tilting back to study the fluorescent lights before rolling in my direction.

"What do we do now, big guy?"

Hate for the wall between us seared through me, but I pushed it back. Shoved it down with all the other unchangeable shit from my life of experiments and captivity.

"Talk."

Her nose, small, pointed, and so different to mine, scrunched in an adorable way.

"About what?"

I shrugged, the movement causing a ripple of pain, reminding me of the damage I'd done to my body. Shame and a tinge of embarrassment filled me.

I'd never cared what anyone thought of them. Of me.

But Daff?

I cleared my throat, my purr fading to a soft thrum. It

hurt like hell from months of abuse. And the talking. I hadn't talked this much in a week, let alone a day in months.

Guilt swamped me at the thought of King watching me deteriorate. Of losing another brother.

With my Angel here, centring me, filling me with peace and a contentment I hadn't known possible, maybe he wouldn't have to anymore.

Hope, and something else I couldn't quite name surged through me.

"Anything." I wasn't above begging her for whatever scraps of herself she was willing to give me.

"I don't…I'm not good at talking."

"Please."

Need roared through me at the flash of her teeth sinking into her bottom lip. All I could see was mine doing the same. Of dragging my tongue along the side of her neck before sinking my teeth into her shoulder, marking her as mine.

"Anything. Right. Okay." She squinted, looking so damn cute. "I'm what you call trailer trash."

The growl escaped me before I could stop it, making her freeze.

"It's okay, Prowl. It's the truth. I'm the third generation to live there, and at the rate I was going, wouldn't have escaped passing it on to another."

She looked away with a sigh. "It's why I'm here. The money means I'll be able to leave that place in my rear-view mirror. I can go to college. Buy a house. Move Dad out and be completely debt free. Finally break the cycle."

"How long?"

"My contract?

I nodded.

"Two years."

That's all I'd have with her? My lungs squeezed, making it hard to breathe, to force my next words out.

"I'm sorry you're trapped here."

With me.

When I already knew, in the depths of my split being, I'd die when she left.

She was the other half of my soul. My calm in the storm. The piece I was missing. My lion needed her. I needed her. Whatever progress I made would be undone when she left.

I wouldn't survive without her.

I didn't want to.

Daff sprang off the couch, stopping just outside my reach, her beautiful eyes gazing up at me.

"Don't be. If I can help you make this," she waved at the wall separating us, "the tiniest bit better for you, it will absolutely be worth it to me."

"You bring my soul peace."

Her body wavered, looking like she wanted to step closer to me before shaking her head and stepping back.

"Lara said this might not last. What if this, me, wears off?"

"I'll still be forever glad I had it."

"Damn, that's sweet."

I'd been made and trained to be the ultimate weapon. Being called sweet should've sounded like an insult.

Coming from her, it meant everything.

She rolled her shoulders, a petite hand gripping the back of her neck.

"Do you mind if I shower? I feel gross from travelling and could really use the hot water."

My body tensed, causing my bruises to ache.

"What's the matter?"

She needed to take care of herself. I wanted her to. I wanted her to have everything she needed to be happy. But the thought of her being out of my sight, of the soap and water masking her scent?

I pushed against my bars, desperate to get closer to her. To not lose this peace, this sanity.

"I need to see you. If I can't smell you or see you, I'll…"

"Think I'm gone?"

"That you were just my imagination."

"What if I keep talking?"

Would it be enough? Or would my bastard of a brain convince me I was only imagining her?

It didn't matter. For her, I'd try. I'd do anything, including letting her go, to live a better, happier life after her contract ended.

"Please."

She nodded. "I can do that."

CHAPTER 4
DAFF

I placed my shampoo, conditioner and soap on the shower ledge, dumped my clean clothes on top of the closed toilet lid, and pulled the privacy curtain along its track, my mind scrambling for a topic.

"Do you have any questions for me?"

Sure, he might ask me something I wasn't completely comfortable answering, but who was he going to tell my answers to?

I'd have a million questions if I were him. I hadn't been told to avoid any particular topics, but that part of our brief might've been covered after they'd returned to conference room two.

"Tell me everything."

My shirt coming off over my head muffled my chuckle. "That's a pretty broad topic."

"Everything about you."

"Right," I mumbled, flipping the water to hot before ditching my jeans and underwear. "We can talk about literally anything. Compared to that, I'm a boring choice."

"Not to me."

I stepped under the spray, a groan escaping me as the hot water hit the tight muscles in my neck and shoulders.

"Daff?"

"Sorry! The hot water distracted me. Ummm. I have two brothers, both older. My dad raised us. He was seriously injured when I was little, and couldn't work. Mum took off about a year later. Said she couldn't carry the family anymore."

His growl cut over the sound of the spraying water.

"Your mother left you?"

I shrugged, forgetting he couldn't see me. "It happens. And it was better than her staying and resenting us. That would've made all our lives miserable."

His growl grew more intense. "It was her duty to stay and care for you. For all of you."

"While it would've been nice, not everyone can handle that level of responsibility."

"I would've stayed."

I paused, something in his voice making my heart thud with the truth of it. "I know." I cleared my throat as I worked up a lather in my hair.

"Steven's the oldest. He has an off again, on again partner and two kids. He helps with Dad's medical bills when he can, but most of his time and money goes to them, which it should.

"Will's next. He means well, but he lets his temper get the best of him, which means he loses more jobs than he keeps.

"Then there's me. I hustled my butt at school, thinking if I got a degree, I could get us out of debt faster, but education costs money and even if I'd scored a full ride, classes and study meant I wouldn't be bringing anything in, on top of losing my wage from after school shifts. Our family was barely scraping by as it was. It sucked letting that dream go, but—"

The sound of a full body slam cut me off.

"Prowl?"

Another slam.

"Prowl!"

I grabbed my towel, flinging it across my body as I dashed out from behind the curtain.

Prowl was breathing hard, his eyes wild.

He fell to his knees at the sight of me, and I rushed forward, stopping just far enough to stay out of reach.

"Oh my god! What happened?"

He drew in a shaky breath. "Your scent was fading, and I couldn't see you."

I fisted my towel tighter, ignoring the shampoo sliding down my neck and the water puddling beneath me. "My voice wasn't enough?"

"I couldn't trust it. Couldn't trust you were still really here."

"I'm sorry."

His butt sank back onto his heels as his eyes ran over me, looking like he was memorising every trailing drip and soap-covered curve.

"We tried."

"Yeah, but I still need to wash this off," I said, waving at myself.

His body tensed. "I need to see you."

"I'll be naked!"

"Please."

"Jesus."

"Please," he repeated, his voice like gravel, rough with a sharp edge of desperation.

I looked back at the running shower. "Maybe I can hang the towel across while I..." I trailed off, realising there was nothing I could attach it to, or use to keep it high enough to cover my bits.

I was too soaped up to put anything back on, and seriously didn't want to spend the next two years showering in my underwear.

Which meant one thing.

Prowl was going to see me naked.

He wouldn't be the first, and he most likely hadn't seen enough women to judge me too harshly on my stretch marks and dimpled thighs. Plus, he probably wouldn't get much further than staring at my boobs.

I nodded, more to myself than him, as I walked back to the shower.

Prowl wasn't asking for a show. He was asking for help staying calm, and helping him was what I was here for.

"Have you met many other women?"

"The ones they've brought here, trying to help me," he said, his voice still rough.

I swallowed. "Any naked ones?"

"Just porn," he said, matter-of-factly.

My eyes flew back to him, where he still hadn't moved. Two new angry welts were already appearing where his body had met the wall.

I reached for the curtain, wondering how far I could keep it pulled closed. Did he just need a glimpse of me every now and then? Or did he need a constant, full view?

My thighs clenched at the thought, pulling a groan from me. The poor guy was just trying to keep his sanity, and here I was, getting a tingle in my bits over the idea of being watched.

I cleared my throat as I dragged the curtain the whole way open. Prowl had enough damage to his body without me causing more.

"Do you still need me to talk?"

I braced for his answer. I didn't think I could manage both, but I'd stumble through whatever I needed to.

He shook his head, thank god.

I took a steadying breath, gave my thighs one last inappropriate squeeze, then dropped my half-soaked towel and stepped beneath the still-running water.

I tipped my head back, drowning my hair with closed eyes. I could feel his gaze like a physical heat, touching every part of me.

The tingle turned into an ache, and my nails running over my scalp, removing the last of my shampoo added to the intensity.

My eyes fluttered open as I stepped clear of the spray, squeezing the water from my hair. Prowl was standing again, his hands gripping his barred door, watching me slide the conditioner through my dark strands.

"You okay, big guy?"

He inhaled through his nose, a flash of frustration crossing his face, there and gone again in a blink. I took the following dip of his chin as a yes.

"Of course you are," I said, soaping up my wash cloth.

My voice sounded normal, but my breaths were quick and shallow, and I could feel the beat of my heart thumping in both my chest and my clit.

The cloth started at my neck, before working its way along my shoulders and down each arm. Prowl's breath caught in his throat, loud enough for me to hear, as I lathered my breasts, stomach and inner thighs.

He growled, and my nipples hardened in response, the low tone vibrating through me like a physical touch.

I gathered enough courage to look at him, but his eyes were glued to my body, the tent in his pants reassuring me it wasn't a panicked sound.

I turned my back to him, biting back a whimper as his

rough tone grew louder. I dropped the cloth, my hands running over my skin, lingering a little too long in places, my mind shoving images of him standing behind me, replacing my slim fingers and soft palms with his thick, roughened ones.

My clit responded with a desperate throb.

I knocked the temperature to freezing, releasing a startled gasp as it hit my skin, helping me crash back to reality. But it was hard to forget when my body still ached with need.

Thirty seconds more and the water was off, my wet towel trying and ultimately failing to do much besides remove the bulk of the water from my hair, the still dry second towel wrapped securely around me.

The door alert sounded and opened a few seconds later, revealing a guard in fatigues and a woman in a simple blue uniform pushing a kitchen trolley.

The guard looked between us. "Dinner's here."

The woman gave me a nervous smile before putting a covered tray and a condensation-covered jug on my dining table. She didn't acknowledge or even glance in Prowl's direction, which sent of spike of anger through me.

He was still a person. One who'd obviously been struggling. Whatever her past visits had been like, he was securely contained and clearly calm. She had no reason to be ignoring his existence.

She took the cover off a second tray and passed the guard the paper plate beneath, loaded with way too much meat and not nearly enough veggies, along with three empty paper cups.

"Is it alright for me to approach, Prowl?"

Prowl's eyes raked over him before settling back on me. He took a few steps back, clearing his doorway.

"I'm good."

The guard covered the distance in quick strides, placing his food and cups on the small ledge that sliced through the midpoint of his barred door before stepping back beside the woman.

"The kitchen will collect your dishes when they deliver breakfast."

"No dessert?" Popped out before I could stop it.

The guard quirked an eyebrow. "There usually is. Kara?"

The woman in blue shrugged. "I just push the trolley."

He rolled his eyes at her answer. "I'm Henry."

"Daff," I said, giving an awkward wave.

"Nice to officially meet you. I'm your first responder tonight. Not that she'll need to hit that button, will she Prowl?"

The left side of Prowl's wide nose flared, but his eyes stayed on me. "I'll keep her safe."

Henry raised an eyebrow but didn't comment.

I didn't appreciate his reaction to Prowl's answer, but I got it. How could he possibly keep me safe from behind his bars, and eight inches of wall?

"I'll be out there if you need me."

"Okay," I answered, as he guided Kara out and closed the door.

I wanted to ask Prowl if all the women he'd met treated him like that, but I didn't want to upset him again, and I wasn't sure I wanted to know the answer.

"Henry seems nice."

Prowl grunted, watching me as I dressed like fire was chasing me, which was ridiculous since he'd just seen me wash every inch of my body. I sat at the dining table and uncovering my food, a smaller version of his, but with a better ratio of vegetables.

"Are you going to eat?"

He was eyeing his food like it might attack him.

"I've not felt hungry in a long time."

I paused, my knife and fork hovering over my steak.

He'd likely lost a lot of muscle mass if he hadn't been eating. Which was nuts. He was easily three of me across and ripped like an airbrushed bodybuilder in a gym magazine.

"Would you try for me?"

His large hand reached for his plate, taking it with him as he sank into a squat and sniffed it.

His eyes flew to mine, his shoulders bouncing in a small shrug.

"Habit. They drugged our food a lot. It was the only way they could briefly immobilise us, besides doing that," he said, flicking a finger towards his neck and the band of scarring I hadn't noticed.

Whether it was the distraction of his facial differences, his beard mostly hiding it, or the onslaught of hormones while I showered and he watched, now that I'd seen the inch-thick scar wrapping all the way around his neck; it was nuts that I hadn't.

"The aftereffects of being drugged are easier to deal with on the waking side if you know it's coming beforehand."

"That's awful."

His shoulders moved again. Did he keep the movement small because his bruises hurt? Or because he thought his past wasn't a big deal?

"It was all we'd ever known."

"It's better here, though?"

The heat in his golden eyes threatened to melt me.

"Better than anything I could have ever hoped for."

CHAPTER 5
DAFF

I shot forward, the blanket falling from me as I grabbed my chest, my heart thumping painfully within. It took a moment to remember where I was, and another to pinpoint what woke me.

Prowl was lying on the bare floor, his body pressed like a second skin against our dividing wall, his forehead digging into the bars at the bottom of his door.

A pained whimper escaped him as he tried to thrash, but with nowhere to go, he only pushed harder against them.

Another thrash, another thump, another whimper.

"Prowl?"

He didn't respond.

"Prowl?" I called, a little louder.

Still no response.

Were you supposed to wake someone up from a nightmare? Was he even having a nightmare? Or was he trapped in a memory?

My voice wasn't helping him, and his eyes were closed, so he couldn't see me. The only other thing I could do to try and soothe him was fill his nose with my scent. But how could I get him to sniff me?

"Damn it!"

I pulled my blanket off my bed and dropped it just out of his reach before following it down. The last thing I needed was a cold ass, and if I moved much closer, he'd be able to reach me. I believed he absolutely meant it when he said he'd never hurt me... but he wouldn't know what he was doing in this state.

"Prowl?" I said again, grabbing my mostly dry hair by the ends and flapping it like an idiot. I mean, how else was I supposed to make myself smell more or push it towards him?

His restlessness slowed for a moment, a brief, fleeting moment, before he thrashed again.

"What the hell do I do now?"

I could only think of one thing. But was I brave enough to do it?

"Shit, shit, shit, shit shitty-shit-shit," I whispered as I crept forward, dragging my blanket with me. "I really hope you meant it, big guy."

Another deep breath and I reached out, slipping my hand through his bars just far enough to touch his broad forehead, where it met with his hairline.

My fingers met a soft layer of velvet fuzz instead of the smooth skin I'd expected.

"Prowl, it's me. I'm here, okay? I won't leave until you're settled, I promise. I really, really don't want you hurting yourself anymore. You've been through enough pain. Not that I have any idea what you've actually been through. The possibilities make me want to puke. You deserve so much better than the life you've been given. All of you do. I—"

His fingers wrapped around my wrist, cutting off my rambling attempt at comfort with a gasp.

He moved my hand, dragging it to his bearded cheek, his body trying to curl forward as if he wanted to wrap his whole being around the place we touched.

His eyes caught the light as they opened, reflecting gold and threatening to incinerate me with their intensity.

"You okay?"

He gave a whisper of a nod before his eyelashes fluttered closed.

I huffed a laugh despite the adrenaline pumping through me, then shook out my blanket one-handed and got comfortable, since it didn't look like he was letting me go anytime soon.

The linoleum floor would be a bitch to sleep on, but I knew, on a level I wasn't comfortable exploring, it'd be worth it.

That he was worth it.

Prowl was on his side, watching me when I woke, cracking my eyes just far enough to not get blinded by the lights turning on.

"Are they on a timer, or does someone hate us?"

"Timer. 7 a.m."

Great. "So no sleep-ins?"

"I won't let them disturb you if you want more."

"Them?"

"Morning med check team."

"You need a team to check you every morning?"

His thumb stroked the inside of my wrist, where he still held my hand to his face.

"I haven't been well."

"I'm sorry."

"Couldn't be helped. They've done what they could, short of knocking me out."

"Lara said that's dangerous for you."

"I'm never out for long."

"Is it like that for all hybrids, or just the lions?"

"The wolves go down the easiest, but there's barely an hour's difference in recovery time between us all."

"Is that why you have that?" I asked, nodding towards the thick band of scaring around his neck.

"The white coats would shock us with enough voltage to make us pass out. If we revived too soon, they'd keep repeating it until they were done."

"I don't know what to say, other than it's a miracle you survived."

He nuzzled my palm.

"I thought I'd been given freedom, only to die here in another prison. You've changed everything for me."

Tears matted my eyelashes, though I did my best to blink them away.

"But what if this calm wears off? I'm terrified for you, of what will happen to you if this doesn't last."

His lips touched my wrist, a whisper of a kiss. I would've thought I'd imagined it if I hadn't seen him do it. "Then I'll make the best of every second it does."

"Last night…"

His fingers squeezed mine. "Thank you. I never dreamed you'd touch me."

"Why not? I mean, yeah, I don't know much about you, but if this goes on for the length of my contract, I'm bound to at some point. Two years is a bloody long time to build trust between us."

His lips parted with his breath.

"We were told not to expect it. That they'd do their best to vet people, but you ultimately couldn't help instinct when confronted with a being as wrong as us."

"Jesus, Prowl! Don't say shit like that! You deserve every single right and privilege the rest of humanity gets.

Happiness, freedom, love, touch, all of it. What the hell have they been telling you?"

"You saw Kara. You saw the women leaving before you. And I've seen a mirror."

"For starters, you were making god-awful sounds and body-slamming the wall when they met you. Of course they were terrified! And Kara can go fuck herself. If she wants to avoid you or pretend you don't exist, that's her issue, not yours."

His lips edged up, hinting at a smile. "You're small and beautiful on the outside, and so fierce and brave on the inside."

I pressed my lips together, doing my best to ignore the flutter in my chest.

"I think you're touch drunk." I wiggled my fingers in his. "I don't think you've held someone's hand this long before, and it's messing with your head."

"The only people who've touched me without gloves are my brothers."

Well, damn. I guess that meant I was going to stay here, holding his hand until my arm fell off. There was no way I was letting go of him now.

My Dad and brothers were never the touchy-feely kind, and I wasn't big on friends, but I'd always wrangled a hug when I needed one.

But to be completely starved for touch your entire life?

It was too awful to think about.

The buzzer went off, warning us someone was about to come in.

"Are you letting me go, or do you want me to stay put?"

"You'd stay?"

I wasn't sure if his question sounded more stunned or hopeful.

"Yeah, big guy, I'll stay here. But I'm going to need to pee at some point."

And poop. In an enclosed space where he'd be able to smell it. Maybe I could convince him to hold his breath until the room aired out.

Prowl let my hand slide from his face but didn't release it as he rolled into a weird crunch and settled on his knees at the edge of his bars, leaving me with enough arm length that I could, very clumsily, pull myself up to sitting. I wriggled on the spot until I could see whoever was about to come through the door.

Lara entered first, followed by Jean, a woman in scrubs and a guy in suit pants and a button down shirt.

Lara froze when her eyes landed on me, her face paling as she noticed my hand, firmly engulfed in Prowl's.

"Release her, Prowl," Jean commanded, raising what looked like a Taser on steroids.

I pulled our joined hands closer to me, hoping he wouldn't mind me yanking on his arm.

"I did this, and I'm okay with it. And he's already checked with me that I'm still okay with it." I turned to Prowl. "You'd let me go as soon as I asked, right?"

It wasn't a question, at least not for me. I knew I could trust him to do what I asked. Though in this case he might fight internally against the loss of touch.

Which would be understandable, considering his history.

"Yes."

"Prove it," Jean said, still aiming his Taser.

A rumble started in Prowl's chest, but I squeezed his hand as hard as I could, jerking his attention back to me.

"Just do it. You can take it again as soon as he's seen. It's not worth the fight or their worry."

His growl broke off, a few seconds passing before he

released me, one finger uncurling at a time like he had to talk himself through it.

"See?" I said, waving my freed hand in front of them. "We good now?"

Jean kept his frown as he re-holstered his weapon. "My job is your safety. There's no such thing as being too careful."

I slipped my hand back into Prowl's, and I swear I could feel his relief it was so strong.

And the med team's discomfort.

"Is that a me and Prowl safety thing? Or a general female-hybrid thing?"

"Both."

"What happens when people start falling for each other and getting physical? You won't be able to point a Taser at every PDA incident that occurs, and you'll be royally screwed once people start having sex. 'Cause that can look wild as hell and still be completely consensual."

Lara and Jean looked at each other.

The half suit glared.

Lara cleared her throat. "We have strict policies in place regarding physical contact. Unless someone is in severe, immediate dangers, hybrids are never to make first contact. This was discussed with your group last night."

"Okay. I can understand that rule, but it still doesn't stop us from touching them first. And don't tell me it won't happen, 'cause it already has," I said, motioning towards our hands.

"We didn't think it was something we'd need to deal with anytime soon."

"And did you think no one on this base would ever want to have sex either?"

The half suit sneered. "They're hybrids."

I grit my teeth. "And you are?"

He straightened his spine, trying and failing to make himself look taller.

"Doctor Lucus Helliot. The most equipped specialist on this base to assess the hybrids dual needs."

I closed my eyes, counting ten Mississippis to calm myself before looking back at Prowl.

"Is this how you got it into your head that no one would ever want to touch you?"

The woman in scrubs stepped towards us.

"I'm Doc Paula, Prowl's physician. What I think Lucus is inelegantly trying to say, is that people will naturally be more disinclined to engage in sexual activities once their specific differences are disclosed."

"I have eyes."

"Yes, but they don't just look different in the obvious, easily seen places. *All* their anatomy is different."

I felt my cheeks heat at her implication, but this wasn't the time for beating around the bush.

"Their dicks are different?"

Doc Paula nodded. "And we're trying our best to minimise the pain of rejection during an incredibly vulnerable moment for the hybrids."

I glanced at each of their faces, and by the looks of it, they all agreed with her.

"You guys aren't into monster smut, are you?"

An even mix of blank looks and furrowed brows answered me.

"Spicy books. Books with explicit sex scenes. Ones that feature everything from shifters to aliens to downright monsters, with their huge, weird dongs and how the human women in them love nothing more than to be railed by them."

Prowl sucked in an audible breath, making me squeeze his hand.

"I'm not calling you a monster. I'm just trying to make them realise there's millions of women out there who read this kind of thing and get off on it. One's who'd be all over you in a heartbeat if they thought you were packing anything like they've read."

I looked back at the four of them, trying not to glare. "You seriously didn't consider this? Because you're in a whole world of trouble if you haven't. I don't know a whole lot about the women who arrived with me, but one thing we all found in common within half an hour of meeting, is our love for spicy sci-fi and paranormal romance."

"We might've misjudged our timeline," Doc Paul said, looking at Lara. "We should give both groups and any other female staff a full rundown on what to expect if they're going to sexually engage with a hybrid. It will lower the risks of unnecessary rejection and possible trauma."

Damn. What kind of cocks were these guys packing? I mean, a trauma response to exposure? What the hell?

"Agreed. Jean?"

"Agreed."

Doctor Lucus the idiot shook his head. "Doing that could potentially encourage sexual activity."

"I'm willing to risk that possibility if the information helps prevent the trauma of unnecessary rejection," Lara said, giving him her full attention. "The hybrids have enough self image issues, don't you think?"

The stare down continued until Doc Paula spoke.

"You're looking better than you have in a long time, Prowl. Have you eaten? Slept? Any new wounds or damage to your body I should know about?"

"He ate all his dinner." And I was pretty damn proud of it, too. I could tell he was only eating to humour me at first, but after those first few mouthfuls hit his stomach, his hunger kicked in and he'd wolfed it down.

Was I allowed to say wolfed? Would the hybrids consider that offensive?

"That's great. And sleep?"

"More than usual." He gestured to the smears of dry blood on the wall. "And no more damage since Daff arrived."

That wasn't quite true. He'd got two decent body slams in during the shower freakout, but I wasn't about to offer that info up. Not when we'd fixed the situation ourselves.

"I'm happy for you, Prowl. That's a lot of progress in an incredibly short amount of time."

"Are you still responding to her scent?" Doctor Helliot asked.

"Yes."

"Compared to voice and touch, how does it rank in calming you?"

"Touch first, voice and scent are interchangeable."

"It depends on the situation?"

"Possibly. We haven't had enough to know."

He motioned towards our joined hands. "How did that happen?"

Prowl's fingers tightened around mine.

"He was restless in his sleep, so I moved closer, trying to get my scent near him. I ended up touching him through the bars. It helped, so I stayed."

He nodded as he jotted it down.

"And Daff, how are you coping with this?"

"It's not what I expected to be doing." Not that I'd had any idea what that would've been, regardless. "But I'm good." I shifted my focus to Jean. "I know I can't leave, but is there a way I could talk to Mandy? I'd like to stay in contact with her."

"I can absolutely make that happen for you."

I sank back closer to Prowl with relief. I couldn't

remember the last time I'd had an actual friend. My life had always been school, helping Dad and work, then eventually just Dad and work. I didn't want to lose the one I'd newly found in Mandy.

"Thank you, Jean."

"If that's everything?" Lara asked the others.

"Bloods, if Prowl's okay with it. It's been a month, and I'd like a full workup. I'm especially interested to see if there's any notable biological changes since calming for Daff. Prowl?" Doc Paula asked.

He nodded, and the arm that wasn't attached to my hand slid through the bars. She approached slowly, making sure he was okay with her proximity before tightening a band around his arm and checking his veins.

She pulled a syringe from her pocket, and I looked away.

"Hold still."

The silence dragged, punctured only by Prowl's deep breaths, pulling my scent into his lungs.

"Done."

I let out a relieved sigh as she stepped away. I freaking hated needles.

"You have no idea how glad I am we could do that the easy way."

My hand clenched his, refusing to loosen until the door closed behind them, their goodbyes floating past my almost unhearing ears.

"What did she mean, the easy way?" I demanded, turning to Prowl.

"No dart or Taser."

"They have no right to do that to you!"

He lifted his free hand, hesitating a fraction from my skin before settling it softly on my cheek, cradling it like it was the most precious thing in the world.

Like I was the most precious thing in the world.

"They were doing what they needed to help me."

"Doesn't matter. They were still knocking you out, just like those other monsters did."

"Helping, not hurting."

I closed my eyes, doing my best to hold back my gathering tears.

"I hate that you lived through that. That pain and fear and god knows what else, was all you knew."

His chest rumbled to life with his purr.

"I'd live through it all again, every second of it, to end up here with you."

"I bet you say that to all the girls you hold hands with."

He huffed what sounded like an almost laugh, his purr getting a little louder as he used his thumb to wipe the tears from beneath my left eye.

"Are these for me?"

"Yes," I whispered.

"Pity, or sadness?"

"Sadness. There might be a few angry ones too."

I don't know if he pulled me closer, if I leant forward, or if it was a bit of both, but we ended up a breath apart, with his lips pressed to my forehead, and me memorising the feeling.

CHAPTER 6
PROWL

She was an angel.

It was the only explanation.

Despite what she said, I was a monster. A merging of species which shouldn't exist, tested and tortured to the brink of my sanity, with enough skill and power to drain life with one hand.

And yet she'd touched me. She'd crawled across the room and slept beside me. She'd given me more hope and peace than I could ever have imagined.

I knew the moment I touched her she was mine, my lips on her skin, sealing my fate to hers.

When she left at the end of her contract, she'd take my heart and soul with her.

And my will to live.

Until then, I'd treasure every second I had with her.

CHAPTER 7
DAFF

We lay on our backs, our fingers tangled through the gap in the bars, and a book in the opposite hand. There'd only been a couple to choose from, and mine was boring as bat shit. An autobiography on some guy I'd never heard of, which read more like a fluff piece for his ego than anything actually noteworthy.

Swapping it had crossed my mind a few times, but I was content where I was and didn't want to disturb Prowl.

He dropped his book to his chest, his head turning in my direction.

"Those books you mentioned."

I cocked an eyebrow at him. "Which ones?"

His fingers drummed on his paperback. "There was only one kind."

"I mentioned Aliens, shifters, monsters in general..." I trailed off, feeling cheeky for playing dumb.

He wriggled, adjusting himself on his blanket. I'd made him get it when I'd got my pillow. He'd huffed over my demand, but he'd done it.

"The sex ones."

"Polite society calls it smut. It sounds less pornographic."

"It's word porn."

I rolled to my side, fully facing him.

"First up; if you tell any female that she's reading porn, she'll get mad at you. Second, it is, and it isn't. There are different levels of spice; by that I mean how descriptive the actual scenes get. Smut can vary from a sweet, one-off scene focused more on emotions than descriptions, to a sexual act every few pages, with extremely explicit, detailed sex."

"Word porn," he repeated, looking at me like I was the one not getting it.

"The biggest difference between the porn you watch and the smut women read is that most of the books are romance. There's an interesting, intentional storyline, and the couple always gets their happily ever after. It's not just meet, fuck, the end.

"There's love, drama, slow burns, emotional angst, character growth, and all the yummy relationship goodness you can think of. Actual porn is just something to watch while you get your rocks off. Most of that shit is completely unrealistic."

Because falling in love with and banging an Alien is completely realistic.

Pot, meet kettle.

In my defence, the hybrids shouldn't theoretically exist, and Doc Paula had pretty much said their lower anatomy wasn't normal so...

Prowl was facing me now, drinking in my words like he'd just sprinted a marathon.

"Rocks off?"

I glanced down at his pants, which looked like they'd shrunk a size, and seriously wished I knew more about what he was packing down there.

"Visual stimulation to orgasm too."

"So, not a good learning resource?"

I didn't even try to stop my snort. "No."

"Are these smut books better?"

"To learn from?"

He nodded.

"The best way to learn is with someone you trust. But as a secondary option... I guess? It would definitely give you a better insight into intimacy then watching porn. Just don't read anything considered dark romance. While it's fun to read, it's not what the average Joe's healthy relationship looks like."

His jaw moved, muscles ticking along his bearded cheek as he studied me.

"Okay."

I let out a shaky breath, not sure what I'd been expecting him to say, and feeling...disappointed?

Did I want him to ask me to teach him?

I forced myself to stay focused on his face instead of dropping another quick look at how tight his pants were sitting.

"When was the last time you brushed your hair?"

It looked as wild as he did. It was long enough to fall past his shoulders with a wave that sent it in multiple directions. Small sections had begun to matt, and if he left it much longer, he'd need scissors to get them all out.

"I don't remember."

"Do you have a comb or brush?"

He shrugged. "If I did, they removed it."

I couldn't help my glare. "I know they've been doing their best to keep you safe, but that's ridiculous. How are you supposed to take care of yourself? Some of your knots look like they'll be a bitch to get out."

A purr rumbled from him.

"I know what you're doing, mister, and it won't change how I feel about this. I have a brush you can borrow. I'll even do it for you, if you can wash it and work some conditioner through it."

I squinted at his shower. "I can share some of mine if you don't have any."

His lips quirked. "Soap usually does the job."

"If you want me to work those knots out for you, you'll be using conditioner."

His smile faded, deflating my heart. "You'd do that for me?"

"Yeah, big guy, I'll do it for you. Might get a bit awkward doing it around your bars, but we'll manage."

He eyed the ones separating us.

"This wall has been my safety net. I've hated being trapped behind it, but I thought I'd lost the chance of ever leaving it."

"You don't think so anymore?"

"I've never wanted out so badly in my life."

"Do you think it's possible?"

His fingers tightened around mine. "You make everything feel possible."

Until I left. What would happen to him then? Would he end up back where he was two days ago, slowly killing himself? Or would he be able to use me as his new safety net, until he grew strong enough to manage on his own?

Either way, two years from now, he'd be without me. And me without him.

The thought pulled something dark and aching to the surface of my heart, but I shoved it down to the same place I kept my memories of Mum leaving us, my dreams to study, the fear of spending the rest of my life alone and barely scraping to get by.

The buzzer sounded, giving us a few seconds' warning that the door was about to open.

But instead of Kara and her food trolley entering with the guard, it was another lion hybrid.

The same one from yesterday?

It felt like half a lifetime had already passed since entering Prowl's space.

I squeezed Prowl's hand and slipped free, his own hesitating a moment before releasing me. Then we were standing, the two hybrids taking full stock of each other as I stepped to the side, giving them both some room.

"This is my brother, King."

"Nice to meet you, King."

King dragged his eyes from Prowl to look me over the same way he'd done his brother.

He was slightly bigger than Prowl. His muscles thicker, shoulders wider, his face more feline, with a flatter nose, larger cheekbones, and thin, brown lips.

An air of sadness clung to him. Which was understandable, considering the life they'd lived before now, and the state Prowl had been in for so long.

"I was just telling Prowl I'd lend him my brush and conditioner if he let me have a go at detangling his hair." I turned to Prowl. "What's your thoughts on facial hair?"

His lips quirked. "No thoughts."

I swung back to King, noting his hair-free jawline, and trying to picture Prowls the same way. "Maybe we just tidy it up."

I hated the thought of Prowl changing. He suited his edge of wildness.

"Thank you for saving my brother."

My fingers tapped against my thighs, struggling with his thanks.

"I haven't done anything except be here."

His assessing gaze went back to Prowl. "I haven't seen you this well in a long time." His head tilted to the side. "Mentally. You could do with more food and rest."

"Daff's given me more than I could have ever dreamed of."

"I really haven't done much."

The closest thing to a glare crossed Prowl's face, sending a shiver down my spine. Fear? Lust? Or a bit of both?

"You've shared your scent with me. Talked to me. Remained where I could always see you. You calmed my sleep with your touch and stayed with me while I slept."

I swallowed against the thick lump forming in my throat.

King's head whipped in my direction. "You touched him?"

"Nothing else was working, so..." I finished with a one-shouldered shrug. "It wasn't a big deal."

King stepped towards me but immediately stopped at Prowl's growl.

He held out his hand, palm first. "Easy, brother. I won't move any closer to her. You have my word."

The sound eased off, but the new tension in his shoulders didn't. Satisfied with Prowl's response, King turned his attention back to me. "We were told never to expect..."

"Female contact?"

He nodded.

"I know. And I'm furious they said that."

Prowl gripped his bars, leaning towards his brother. "There are books called smut. They focus on romantic relationships and detailed sex between monsters and human Women. And Women enjoy reading them."

King's eyes went wide at the information. "They like that?"

"They Love it," I said, making sure I caught Prowl's eyes. "And I thought I made it clear you aren't a monster."

He actually rolled his eyes at me!

"Daff thinks they're a better method for learning about sexual encounters than porn."

"What I actually said, was it's best to learn with someone you trust. But if it's between reading smut and the videos you find online, then yes. Read the smut. Just stay away from dark romance until you have some experience under your belt."

"Experience?"

"Yes, experience. There are women out there who'd bang you both in a heartbeat. There's bound to be some who end up here. I told them this when they checked on us this morning."

King nodded. "I'll visit the library and see if they have any. If not, they'll have to order it in."

"There's a chance that's already been done." I shrugged at the look Prowl gave me. "By the women I arrived with."

King blinked rapidly before clearing his throat.

"Bring me one," Prowl said.

It was more of a demand, but King didn't seem to mind.

"And me, if there's enough."

God knows I'd need a half-decent book to read, with no TV and the boring few we had here.

Prowl's body stiffened like an electric bolt had run through him, and it was all I could do to hide my smirk.

"I'll make sure of it," King said, before motioning towards my bed. "I'll keep Prowl company while you rest."

I felt my nose wrinkle. "I'm good, thanks."

A shadow of a frown crossed his features. "You're not tired?"

"No," I answered, looking between them.

Was I missing something obvious?

"Why would I be?"

"Because you spent your night calming my brother with your touch."

"Ye-e-es. But I just slept on the floor beside him."

His mouth fell open, flashing sharper than usual incisors.

"You slept beside him? While touching him?"

Ooof. His genuine shock felt like a solid punch to the gut.

"There was still a solid wall between most of us, but yeah, I did."

"Why?"

Prowl sucked in a breath.

"Because he needed me to."

King closed his eyes. They were on Prowl when he opened them. "It appears it's not just you she's giving hope to."

He fell into a crouch, and with a searching look in my direction, Prowl followed. I pointed to the shower behind me.

"Do you think you could handle me having a shower while King's with you?"

Prowl's eyes lingered a moment, no doubt replaying last night's one in his mind.

"You've got this, big guy. I'll step right out if you need me."

Though he wouldn't be getting the naked rinse-off version if King was still here. Him, I could handle watching me... anyone else was a hard no.

Which was ridiculous. Rationally speaking, I barely knew the guy. But my gut worked on a whole different level —one that said Prowl was mine to care for. That I could trust him, that he was, in a strange way, mine.

Which was a totally crazy thing to think.

Prowl dipped his chin, which I took as a yes.

"Great. I'll leave you two to catch up."

Neither one of them spoke as I gathered my stuff and pulled the privacy curtain across. Then the water was running, and I had no chance of hearing them.

CHAPTER 8
PROWL

King waited, watching me as I followed Daff's every move, right until she pulled the curtain along its track and turned on the water.

"I never expected to see you like this again."

I gave him a crooked smile. "Sane?" I shook my head, my eyes tracking back to Daff's shower curtain. "Neither did I."

"Do you want to be released?"

It was easy to assume the sadness clinging to him was my fault. There were only three of us left, and Rage, though physically well, had a broken mind. His lion had risen too close to the surface, and he often lost the fight. If King had one of us back...

"I think anything's possible, with Daff by my side. I—"

I broke off, the thought of seeing the open sky, feeling the warmth of the sun on my skin, the wind rush past me as I run, pushing past the burn in my thighs and the pressure in my lungs...

Such simple things, too often taken for granted.

Things I never thought I'd feel again, as sleep slowly deserted me, the need to eat faded, my body dying faster than it could heal.

King motioned towards the shower. "She's nothing like they told us."

"No," I said, feeling the fist around my heart squeeze.

I swear I could see her through the curtain, see the water rolling down her curves, touching all the places I could only dream of.

"Do you think there are others like her?"

I dragged my eyes back to him, grateful I could rest my arms on my thighs, hiding the steel in my pants, trying to spring free.

"You've met more than I have."

King shook his head. "The first group barely interacts with us. They keep to the places they feel safe and never instigate."

"And Daff's group?"

"We haven't met them yet, not officially. We've seen them on the bus and being shown the shared spaces. Tomorrow, I hope."

"Daff has a friend, Mandy. she asked to remain in contact with her. If she's one of the brave ones, I'll ask if she'd be willing to meet you."

King nodded but didn't seem as eager as I'd expected. "I'm glad you found her. And your peace again."

My palm found my chest, rubbing the place where I could feel my heart beat the strongest. "I feel her here. As steady and sure as my heart's beat."

King leant forward, his hand barely pausing before reaching past the bars to land on my shoulder.

"Be careful, brother. She can't stay."

My eyes flashed fire, possessive heat searing through my veins as a growl ripped through me.

"She will always be mine."

King rose and stepped back, his air of sadness returning.

"Then in a way, a piece of her will remain with you, long after she's gone back to her real home."

The shower stopped, and King lowered his voice.

"We've survived pain before. We'll do it again, if needed."

My growl tore free, following him from the room, until the door thunked back into place.

I pressed my head to my bars, pushing until I felt the first bite of pain.

King was right. She wouldn't, couldn't stay. Not forever. She had a home and life out there, and with the money she'd earn from being here, she'd be able to have the life she longed for.

She deserved it.

She deserved anything and everything that would bring her joy.

And if I was lucky, which I hadn't ever believed before her, I might bring her some too.

Daff's head popped through the curtain.

"You okay?"

My purr answered her, needing to reassure her. She shot me a crooked smile as she stepped out, wearing pants that were glued to her like a second skin, a sleeveless shirt that flashed toned arms, and her dark hair pulled up in a messy pile atop her head.

She was the most beautiful thing I'd ever seen.

"You like them?" she asked, doing a spin, briefly flashing her perfect ass in my direction. "They're called leggings. Bit different to your cargos. These are way more comfortable."

If she was hinting I should try them, there wasn't a chance in hell I'd do it. They could feel like feathers cushioning my balls, but there'd be no hiding the steel in my pants any time she touched me.

Or I remembered how she looked, like a wet goddess, naked and glistening in the shower.

She smirked in my direction like she knew where my thoughts had gone.

"Thank you for talking with King."

She cocked her head to the side. "I know to you that seems like a big deal, but it's really not. Not to me, at least. Or anyone else who's a half-decent human being."

This woman.

She was too good for the likes of me.

But I was too selfish not to grasp hold of every possible second I could with her.

Her perfect tits bounced as she raised herself onto her tiptoes and fell again.

"I really hope they figure out a way for me to talk to Mandy. Not that I don't love our little corner of The Compound or my time with you, but I'm keen to know what they've told her about you guys and what they're expecting of the other women."

"I'd like to know too."

"Then let's hope we hear from her soon."

The door buzzed, giving us our incoming warning, before the on-duty guard stepped through, followed by Kara and the trolley with our lunch.

CHAPTER 9
DAFF

Banging on the dark window above the couch made me jerk and Prowl growl.

"It's all good, big guy," I said, which was half true.

I still felt like I was about to puke up my heart, but at least I hadn't shit myself. Which was becoming a growing concern since I'd been needing to for the last two hours, but I couldn't figure out how that was actually going to happen. Because even if I could close the curtain or make Prowl turn his back, he'd still be able to SMELL it.

Peeing had been fine. I could do that easily enough while keeping decent once I could relax enough to let it out. But pooping... ugh. I think my time putting it off was almost up.

"Is that your friend?"

I focused on the now clear window and sprang to my feet, Prowl barely hesitating before freeing my hand.

Mandy had a phone in her hand, eyes flicking between Prowl and I as she fidgeted with the cord connecting it to the wall.

I picked up the one on my side.

"You came!"

"Yup," she said, her eyes darting behind me again. "How're you doing? Wait, can he hear me?"

I half spun towards Prowl, who was watching me with an intensity that if I hadn't spent the last twenty-four hours with, would have made me nervous.

I raised an eyebrow at him. "Can you?"

He raised one back, and I rolled my eyes. "Can you hear Mandy when she talks?"

"Yes."

Damn, that was good hearing.

"That's a yes," I repeated, turning back to her.

She hummed, her eyes dropping to her fingers before brightening. "I've got it. Mouth the words yes or no. Okay?"

"Okay... why?"

She shot me a look that basically asked if I was stupid. "Just do it. It'll help me feel better."

"Okay."

"Good. Question one. Are you okay in there?"

My heart gave an extra thump. Was this what it was like having a friend?

Yes.

"Question two. Do you feel safe?"

Prowl gave a low growl, as if she'd insulted him.

"She's allowed to ask, Prowl. I know you wouldn't do anything to hurt me, but she doesn't."

Yes, I mouthed to her with an eye roll.

"I was going to ask if he'd hurt you, but I guess it'd be pretty obvious if he had. So, question three. Are they keeping you here against your will or making you do anything you don't want to do?"

"No, and no."

"You were supposed to mouth that back to me, so I know you aren't lying!"

"I'm not, and I'm fine, I promise. Prowl's a big teddy bear —teddy lion? With me. I promise."

"Good. I'm glad." Her eyes slid behind me, staying longer this time. "He isn't like the other girls said."

"We all look crazy when we're extremely upset."

"True." She checked out the rest of our room. "There's really not much privacy, is there?"

"No," I said with a snort.

"And the place would give a lot less... I'm not sure how to word this? Torture chamber vibes? If all the dry blood was cleaned off the wall."

I hadn't really looked at it. I'd been too focused on Prowl, and most of that time had been spent at the bars of his door. But now that she'd said it, all I could see were the dry, dark smears of his blood.

It looked utterly gruesome.

Prowl cleared his throat. "If someone brings me some cleaning supplies, I'll clean it up."

"Thanks, big guy. I think that's a great idea. Did you hear that?"

Mandy shook her head but looked intrigued.

"If someone can get us some cleaning supplies, Prowl will take care of it."

Her eyes widened. "Yeah?"

I nodded. "He's good, Mandy. You don't need to worry about me being with him, I promise."

She nodded, looking like she was starting to believe me.

"My turn for questions. What have you been up to? What have they told you about the other hybrids? I want to hear everything!"

She rocked up onto her toes, bouncing with excitement.

"No one on the outside would believe even half of it, I swear!"

I grinned. "Tell me."

"We went back to admin and got the rundown on the different hybrids here, and how to interact with them. There's four of them. Lion, panther, wolf and gorilla."

Wow. Good to know.

"The rules are; they aren't allowed to approach us. They have to wait until we go to them, or we clearly call them over. There are massive consequences for them if they instigate any kind of touch. Which, honestly, I'm okay with. They've spent the majority of their life either locked up or learning how to track and kill. It helps me feel a little safer."

"I'm glad."

I was also glad that I'd been the one to instigate the touching between Prowl and I. Despite the fact I'd probably have shit myself if he'd done it first, it meant they wouldn't ever be able to punish him for it.

"Were you there when they told us we were the second group here?" Mandy asked.

"Yeah. We're Group B."

"Even though we're group B, we'll be doing jobs where we interact with them a lot more."

"Like what?"

"I'll be working in their version of a school slash daycare with the cubs!"

"Whoa. The Cubs?"

"Little girls, all lion hybrids. I met them this morning. Daff, they're amazing. And so damn cute. They're all between four and six years old. At least that's their best guess." She lowered her voice, but I wasn't sure if it'd be enough to stop Prowl from hearing. "They're the only females, and the only children they've found."

When I looked back at Prowl, his head was bowed forward, firmly pressed against his bars, but he was still watching me.

"We've toured all the shared spaces, got our fingerprints

into the system so we don't need keys, synced our base-issued watches," she said, flashing me her wrist, "and settled into our apartments.

"Is your room nice?"

"Nicer than anything I've rented before. There's two people to an apartment, and we're roomies. I made sure they put us together. We have our own rooms and a functional kitchen we can use if we don't feel like eating in the dining hall."

"Nice."

She wiggled a little, then stilled, eyes flashing behind me before pulling the mouthpiece closer to her lips.

"They called us into another information session before lunch. I got the impression it wasn't one they'd had before."

"Yeah? Why?"

"Because it looked like every female on the base was there."

Now she had me curious.

This time, she whispered. "They wanted to warn us about their cocks, and what to expect if we ever... you know... had any sexy time with them below the waist."

So they had listened to me this morning. And acted fast on it. There was a sizeable chunk of satisfaction in that knowledge.

"And?"

"They're different."

I rolled my eyes, but the confirmation made me squeeze my thighs.

"That's not the slightest bit helpful."

She smirked at me.

"Some have spines on them, Daff. Spines!"

Sweet baby Jesus. Who the hell would want that inside them? No wonder they'd been worried about us being unprepared for their cocks.

"Like, sharp ones?"

"God, no! They said they're firm, but soft. Like what you feel when you push the tip of your nose." She did it like she needed to show me.

My fingers itched, wanting to copy her and remind myself what it felt like. And what it would feel like, attached to a cock and moving inside me.

And if that cock happened to be Prowls?

I barely suppressed my shiver.

"How did they take it?"

Had the women been terrified like the doctor predicted, or had they reacted like I'd expected?

"Some of them looked stressed, but most of us, I think, were more than okay with it."

She leaned closer, like she was about to share a secret with me despite the window between us.

"I think we shocked them with our interest in trying the different ones out."

If different hybrids wielded different cocks, which ones had the firm but soft spines that would feel like the tip of my nose when I pressed on it?

I cleared my throat, doing my best not to rub my thighs together, as Prowl started purring behind me. I spared him a glance, wondering what had set him off since the only other times he'd done it was when he thought I was stressed or upset.

"I wonder if the hybrids have had the safe sex talk."

Yeah, I highly doubted it, considering they fully believed no one would ever even want to touch them.

"Can you imagine what their condoms must look like?" She continued. "Or how they worked out the right shape in the first place?"

"I'm sure it's something they'll figure out real quick if they haven't yet."

Prowl's purr went up a notch, enough for Mandy to hear on her end of the line.

"Is he... purring?"

"He doesn't like me being anxious or upset."

"Are you?"

"Not right now, no," I said with a frown, shooting him another look.

Mandy checked her watch. "I gotta go. I'm spending time with the cubs this afternoon and I don't want to be late." She placed her free hand on the window. "I'm really glad you're okay. And that he's not like how he was when we got here."

"Me too. Thanks for coming, Mandy."

"All good. I'll stop by again tomorrow. Bye!"

She hung up her receiver, and must have pressed something else because the window fell dark. I returned my phone to its cradle, then turned to face Prowl.

"Wanna tell me why you're purring?"

His lips lifted into the closest thing I'd seen to smile from him.

"You."

"I'm not sad or stressed," I said, taking measured steps towards him. "So, how can it be for me?"

"*Because of*," he said, closing his eyes as he inhaled me into his lungs.

He looked so damn good doing it.

"Not *for*."

"Oh?" I asked, feeling a little breathless.

The gold in his eyes sparked hotter.

"Your scent changed."

"My scent?"

"Mmm," he rumbled, the sound begging for a whimper from me.

"That," he growled, his lips parting as if he was trying to taste, not just smell the air.

Shit.

The only thing that'd changed was me being seriously turned on. Could he actually scent that?

I stopped just beyond his reach, my heart pounding and pussy aching as I took in the physical size of him.

Sure, he wasn't as big as King, but he'd been wasting away for months. Despite that, he was still a giant wall of muscle, his abs rippling with every breath, and whatever kind of cock he was packing, straining against his pants.

"You're killing me, sweetheart."

"At least it's a better death than the one chasing you before." I clapped a hand over my mouth, meeting his eyes in horror. "I am so freaking sorry I said that. I shouldn't have—"

He pressed his chest to the bars, forcing himself as close as physically possible without reaching for me, his purr rumbling louder, wrapping me in its vibrations.

"I'd choose this end every time."

"Fuck," I whispered, grabbing hold of the bars next to his white-knuckled hands.

Still, he didn't reach for me.

"Prowl—"

The buzzer sounded, and I sprang back, spinning towards whoever was about to come in.

Henry entered with a bucket, a limp rag hanging over its edge.

"Cleaning supplies. Do you need anything else?"

Besides new underwear and a less frustrated clit?

"We're good," Prowl confirmed.

The guard ditched the bucket and left.

I cleared my throat. "You should clean your wall."

Which was actually pretty awful. It was a visual history of the damage done to his body.

It was also a great idea, in theory, to give us some time, if not space, to cool off. Until he reached through the bars and took the cloth, and I realised, I'd be watching him in all his upper naked glory, abdominals shuddering, biceps flexing, the look of steady concentration on his face as he sprayed the wall down and followed it in smooth, circular strokes.

God, to be on the receiving end of that kind of attention. Of those movements focused solely on my body.

Said movements slowed, the gorgeous bastard smirking at me as I realised he'd finished, and was waiting to see how long it took me to stop drooling over him and notice.

Damn him.

"That clean enough for you?"

"Yep. Yes. It looks much better."

He tossed the dirty cloth back through the bars and into the bucket.

"My turn."

"Yours?" I squeaked.

"To get clean."

I popped to my feet, grabbing my shampoo and conditioner, and passing it through to him.

"Two shampoos, one condition. Work the conditioner through as best as you can with your fingers, then let it sit for a few minutes before rinsing it out."

"And you'll brush it for me?"

"Yeah, big guy. I'll brush it for you."

Between one blink and the next, he'd turned on the water and was undoing the top button of his pants.

"Stay where I can see you."

I nodded, not trusting my voice as he turned around and dropped his pants.

I doubt I could peel myself away if I wanted to.

His head tipped back, the hot water dragging a satisfied groan from him.

I closed my eyes, but he was already etched into the back

of my eyelids, his perfect ass clenching and releasing along with the rest of his muscles as the heat of the water worked its magic.

I focused on my breathing as I listened to him move. Opening and closing bottle lids. The water falling harder and softer, depending on how much of his skin it was hitting as he moved around. Washing his hair. His body.

"Look at me."

The command made my clit throb.

"You need to be able to see me. I don't have the same excuse."

"Look. At. Me."

He stood like a god, legs spread, eyes hooded, his right hand mapping the muscles of his abdomen as it slid lower. I watched, thighs clenched, clit throbbing, as his fingers finally stopped, wrapping around the base of his cock.

He was too far away, the spray of water misting the view of his thick fingers stroking in a slow, steady twist, blocking the details I was on the verge of begging for.

He inhaled like his life depended on it, his loud purr following, his hand picking up speed.

"Daff."

It was half warning, half plea, and there was no stopping the whimper that escaped.

"Fuck."

Another deep inhale and he came, the guttural sound he made sending shivers through me.

Is that what he'd sound like, coming inside me? Or would it sound even better, knowing it was my body that had wrung it from him, my muscles that had gripped and stroked him, and not just his hand and the fantasy of it?

I forced myself to look away, punishing my bottom lip, as he washed himself off and turned off the water.

He cleared his throat, snapping my head back in his direction.

He was already dressed, wearing joggers that sat low on his hips; the odd drip falling from his hair, landing on his shoulder before sliding down the indents of his chest.

My lips ached to trace their path. I'd give almost anything to crawl through those bars and catch them with my tongue.

I blinked at the mental image. How the hell had I gotten in so deep, so fast with him? No guy had ever pushed my buttons like this. Or had me wanting him to push my buttons like this, so to speak.

"You alright, Angel?"

Was that regret in his voice? Or worry?

"Yeah." I licked my drips lips, forcing myself to swallow. "I'm good. You?"

His shoulders dropped, replaced by a much more confident-looking smirk.

"Much better."

I picked up my brush, my rolling eyes hard to miss as I met him at the bars.

His nervousness was back. "How do we do this?"

"Turn around and sit close to the bars. I'll slip my hands through and brush it that way."

A nod and he settled in place. I followed him down, my legs crossing as I wriggled as close as I could.

My knees stopped me from getting close enough to be comfortable.

"Hang on."

I slipped one foot between the bars, then the other, then slid forward as far as my thighs would let me.

Prowl's back was a tense wall until I stilled.

"Are you okay like this? I couldn't get close enough and

still be comfortable the other way, which is a biggy since I'll be here a while."

He cleared his throat, his fingers gently wrapping around my right ankle, suffusing it with warmth I felt all the way to my belly.

"I'll always be okay with whatever you want to do with me."

My hand replacing his, wrapping around his cock, stroking him, flashed through my mind, forcing a chuckle from me.

"I bet you say that to all the girls."

His fingers tightened a fraction. "Only ever you, Daff."

I gathered his hair, so much longer now that it was wet, and sectioned off a tangled chunk at the base of his neck. The hair tie from my wrist held the rest up in a man bun.

Anyone seeing us right now would think we were nuts. Or rather, I was. I was pushed up against the bars, my thighs squished between them, my legs resting on either side of a giant lion hybrid. Said hybrid, sat with his head tipped back, a content rumble vibrating from him, despite the amount of knots I snagged, and slowly teased free.

We'd been there a while, not that I was making any effort to get through his hair that fast, not with how much he was enjoying it, and if I was being completely honest with myself, how much I was, too, when I broke our silence.

"Do you think they'll ever let you out of there?"

"I need you more than I need to be out from behind this wall."

What if he could have both?

Was I crazy for thinking it? For risking it?

"What if they let you out—" his body tensed, his fingers still looped around my ankle tightening, "—with me still here with you. Do you think they'd let us try?"

"I would never hurt you, Daff. I'd hurt myself before I

ever did that. But I don't want you doing something you're not comfortable with or ready for. Having you here is enough for me."

"I'm not sure it's enough for me."

A genuine groan escaped him. "I'd cut off my left nut to be on the other side with you."

"I—"

The door buzzed.

Prowl's back tensed, but I didn't stop. We weren't doing anything wrong, and I'd just point-blank told him I trusted him enough that they could remove his damn wall from between us, and I'd be fine with it.

The only real trust issue I had was with myself, and whether I could keep my hands and mouth—and I might as well add the rest of my body parts—to myself.

The shift must have changed, because a different guard followed Kara in with her dinner trolley, along with Jean, who took a moment to collect himself at the sight of us.

I spoke before he could. "Prowl washed his hair. I'm getting his knots out."

"I can see that."

I nodded as I continued with my brush strokes, making sure none had slipped past me.

"Who do we need to talk to about letting Prowl out of there?"

"I don't think it's a good idea to remove you from his presence yet. It might be a substantial amount of time still, before you can—"

"I didn't say anything about me leaving him."

Clearly, I'd surprised him. And Prowl, if his shallow breathing and grip on my ankle was anything to go by.

I know we'd only just broached the subject, but if it took a while to convince the higher-ups, we should get the ball rolling now.

I paused, resting one hand on Prowl's shoulder, the other pointing at Jean with my brush.

"Obviously, I'm comfortable with him. He's had more than enough opportunities to harm me—"

Prowl's angry growl cut through the room. I patted him where I touched him.

"I know you wouldn't; I'm just pointing out the obvious." I looked back at Jean. "What do we need to do to let him out?"

"My job is your safety, Daff, I don't know if—"

"Nope. I'm asking what we need to do, not your opinion on it. At the end of the day, it's my choice, and I want to know the steps we need to take to make it happen. Can you help us figure them out or not?"

He sighed, a hand scrubbing over his head as he glanced at the guard and back again.

"I'll bring it up with Lara and medical tonight, so we have time to think on it before tomorrow morning's check in. We'll see what everyone thinks and if there's an agreeable plan we can put in motion. IF all parties are on board with the plan, including me, about the measures put in place to keep you safe."

"Thank you, Jean. Was there anything else?"

Another shake of his head. "I just wanted to check in with you. I'll leave you both to your dinner."

"Jean?"

"Yes?"

"Thank you for sending Mandy by. I appreciate it."

"You're welcome."

The door closed behind them, and Prowl lifted my leg, making me squawk in surprise as he pressed a kiss to the inside of my ankle.

CHAPTER 10
PROWL

She wanted me.

This sweet, brave goddess wanted me.

She'd calmed with me her touch. Watched me have the most intense orgasm of my life, climbed as far as she could through those damn bars to brush my hair, and told me she trusted me.

And I believed her.

How could I not, when she'd asked Jean for a plan to release me?

While she stayed with me.

Goddamn fucking miracles, every single one of them.

The best one of all?

The scent that had crawled inside my soul, giving me the hardest dick of my life, one that still refused to completely go down.

Her arousal. For me.

I'd die a happy male with that scent in my nose.

The half-mast in my pants throbbed, and I sucked back a groan, refusing to disturb her.

My Angel.

My Daff.

Because she was mine. Even if this was all there ever was between us.

"You okay, big guy?"

Her fingers tightened in mine with her question, her voice rough with sleep.

"Never better."

"That's not saying much about your experiences before now."

Daff covered her yawn with her free hand, stretched out her toes, then snuggled back into her pillow.

She was sleeping on the floor with me again, but this time I'd made sure she was comfortable, making her take both my pillow and blanket despite her protests.

"They'll be here soon."

She cracked an eyelid, just far enough to study me. "Are you nervous?"

"No."

Her cute little nose scrunched. "But this could be your next step out of here, and if they say no—"

"I have you, Daff. You're all I need."

She wriggled closer. "What about your brothers? What do they need?"

An unsettling heaviness washed over me.

Because she was right.

King was... not himself. He wore worry and sadness like a permanent weight vest, and with Rage lost to his instincts... I was all he had left.

I drew her hand to my lips, kissing her fingers.

"I want more for you than this," she whispered. "You deserve so much more than this. You all do." She grinned, her seriousness dropping. "I got your back, Jack. Whatever happens."

My gut sank, my abs clenching against the sickening feeling.

"You want to call me Jack?"

Her eyes widened as she jerked my hand to her chest, close enough to feel the rapid beat of her heart through the soft swell of her breasts.

"Fuck no! It's just a saying. I don't even know where it comes from. It's just something people say when they mean, they won't let you down. I don't want to change your name. I wouldn't change a single thing about you, Prowl."

She looked so damn earnest I knew she meant every word.

"I believe you."

"Oh, thank god." She took a deep breath, but whatever she was going to say stopped with the sound of that fucking buzzer.

"We should probably stand for this. We'll look more serious than curled up on the floor like kids looking up at their parents."

She let go of my hand as she stood, tossing the bedding back where it belonged before coming back, slipping her hand behind her so we were still touching when they came in.

Jean led the way, followed by Lara, Doc Paula, the jerk-off zoologist with a human psychology degree - Lucus Helliot - who I truly believed thought he shit pure sunshine. The on-duty guard brought up the rear, remaining by the door.

I held back a growl as they all visually checked over Daff first, making sure she was fine. Which rationally, I appreciated. It would've pissed me off if they'd dismissed her health and wellbeing for mine. But I hated the implication that they needed to check her in the first place.

They couldn't see our connected hands, but noted how close we stood.

Jean cut to the chase.

"I alerted everyone to your request, and we met this morning to discuss it."

"And?" Daff asked, standing a little taller.

Her thumb stroked my skin where our hands touched.

God, this woman.

If they let me out, and she wanted me like I believed? There wasn't a chance in hell I would hesitate in making her mine.

Daff's scent may have been the one to break through my raging instincts enough to grasp my sanity, but it was her I wanted. Every inch of her pale skin, every dark hair on her body, every breathy moan that passed my angels lips.

I'd claim them all 'til my dying breath, or however long she let me.

"Any relapses? Depression, rage or disassociation?" Doc Paula asked.

"No."

"Daff?" she asked, looking for confirmation.

"None."

"Suicidal ideation, thoughts or desires to self-harm or harm those around you?"

If they thought for one fucking second I would ever consider harming Daff—

"No," she said, stilling my building rage, the steady stroke of her thumb helping me focus past it.

"We need to hear it from him."

That, from Helliot.

"No," I snapped, barely suppressing a growl.

Doc Paula continued, unbothered by my tone. "I noted a significant biological change in yesterday's bloods. I'd like to take a second sample to confirm, and continue regular draws to track any other changes."

Hopefully, those changes were a good thing. As for the bloods? I nodded like the choice was mine.

"We need to speak with Daff privately," Lara said, as Doc Paula cinched a tie around my arm.

Daff's fingers clamped around mine like a vice, as panic sucked the air from my lungs.

"I'm not going anywhere."

Lara pointed to the dark window. "You'll still be able to see each other. It won't take—"

Daff cut her off.

"I said no. Anything you need to say about Prowl or our next steps, will be said in front of both of us."

My purr exploded into the room, widening the eyes glued to us.

"You hear that? That's for me. I know what you're thinking, what you're worried about, but Prowl won't hurt me. I trust him, and he trusts me."

She sounded so damn proud saying it.

"Do you trust him with your life?" Jean asked. "Because that's what will be on the line. Whatever answer we give, whatever plans we put in place, it's ultimately you who risks the most doing this."

My woman didn't flinch. "One hundred percent."

Jean looked resigned, Lara looked worried, Doc Paula looked unaffected and Doc Jerk-off...looked less than impressed.

Daff's head swivelled between them. "What's the verdict?"

Everyone looked at Jean, who was still studying her like he was trying to see under her skin.

"Are you absolutely sure about this, Daff?"

He held up his hand, stopping her protest.

"He's right to ask," I said, startling her into looking at me.

I held her gaze, needing her to take this seriously. "I would never, ever, willingly or otherwise hurt you."

"I know. I'd be telling everyone to fuck right off if I didn't believe in you."

"That doesn't mean we need to do this now. Or ever."

She took a deep breath, filling her lungs and stopping my heart.

I'd meant what I said. I'd stay on this side of my wall forever, happily even, as long as she stayed with me.

But the ways I could worship her without it separating us?

"We're doing this." Her eyes were spitting fire, daring me to argue with her. If I didn't think everyone in the room would worry I'd lost my mind again, I'd roar so fucking loud the stars would hear me.

"Then let them do what they need to do to sign off on it."

Daff took a deep breath and nodded, then turned back to face our visitors.

"I understand the risks," she said, focusing on Jean. "And I'm doing this. What do you guys need from us to make it happen?"

Jean pointed to the steel door. "Two officers out there at all times. They'll have both Tasers and live ammunition. If the situation requires it, clearance to shoot-to-kill has been granted. They will do random, around the clock safety checks, and you will be required to wear a panic button at all times, in case things go sideways."

Daff's grip was threatening to cut off my circulation.

"Is that a yes?" She asked, sounding as desperate as I felt for the verbal confirmation.

"Yes," Lara said, since no one else seemed to want to give the final answer.

She spun to me, her eyes wide. "They said yes!"

I ached to slip my other hand through the gaps and touch her, but now wasn't the time.

"When?" she asked, still looking at me with so much goddamn joy in her eyes.

"We can come back—"

She shot a glare over her shoulder. "Why not now?"

Jean sighed. "You're not going to make my job easy, are you?"

"Nope," she said, a smile lighting her face.

CHAPTER 11
DAFF

I should be terrified.

I mean, my heart was pounding, my chest felt tight, my muscles randomly twitched with an insanely fierce need to move, all of them signs of a massive adrenaline dump.

But I'd felt more nervous last night, begging Prowl to hold his nose for a full ten minutes when my gut had finally revolted and I was forced to give in and do a gloriously satisfying crap. That definitely stank.

Prowl's hand had slid from mine as I followed Jean to the Dining table, but his eyes didn't leave me.

He looked freakishly calm while Lara and Doc Paula took turns speaking and occasionally nodding as the requested vial of blood was drawn.

"Daff!" Jean snapped.

"Sorry."

He shook his head like he was trying to shake off his frustration. "This is too important to zone out on."

I lifted the credit card sized device dangling from my hand. "This goes around my neck. Three seconds of pressure and it'll set off an alarm that will trigger the waiting guards, who will bypass the seven-second door delay and, depending on the level of risk to my safety, shoot to kill. I am never, ever, under any circumstances to remove it from my neck, not even while I'm showering.

"I will also, at all times that I'm wearing clothes, wear the second panic button which will be attached to my waistband and used as a backup device." I flashed him the hip it was already clipped to. "Same deal with the three seconds, door bypass, and kill order."

Doctor Helliot, who'd joined us during Jean's panic button drill, spoke.

"It's not too late to change your mind."

I raised an eyebrow at him. "I'm doing this."

His mouth turned down, but Jean's voice rose above the noise of the room before he could continue.

"Listen up, everyone. Daff's ready, so the next few minutes will go as follows. The room will be evacuated by everyone except Daff, Daniel and Pete. Daniel will open Prowl's door under Pete's supervision.

"When both are satisfied Prowl is in full control of himself, they'll see themselves out, and start the first rotation of random to them safety checks."

His eyes met and held mine, then Prowl's.

"We'll be watching," he said, pointing to the dark window, "As soon as Prowl's door opens, their shoot-to-kill order will be in effect. Understood?"

Prowl's voice rang clear. "Understood."

The med team filed out, the dark window cleared, and the steel door slid closed. Daniel. the guard moving to Prowl's door, looked tense, but the one standing back watching, looked unruffled.

Lara's face was pinched, but she shot me a thumbs-up. Rattling keys broke the silence.

Daniel looked up at Prowl. "You good?" He asked, hesitating with his key a hairsbreadth from the lock.

"I'm good," Prowl answered, his eyes running over the guard before settling back on me, a soft purr filling the space between us.

The key turned, and his door swung wide, its bars no longer between us.

His purr swelled above the noise of my pounding heart.

I wanted this, I absolutely did, but a brief flash of panic, still hit me. Which explained why it took me so so long to realise he hadn't moved.

At all.

Was he worried about taking this step forward only to lose it again?

"Prowl?"

His purr knocked up a level, but he still hadn't so much as blinked.

"I'm okay. You can come out."

His shoulders dropped a fraction, but his rumble didn't.

Slow, measured steps brought him to his open door where he paused, his eyes running over me, scanning for signs that I'd changed my mind or wasn't okay.

His hesitancy was beginning to piss me off.

If he was going to do something, he would've done it the moment his door swung wide. He could have been on me or the guards quicker than we could have blinked.

Not dragging this goddamn moment out, treating me like an explosive about to go off. Which was ironic.

"I trust you."

Those steady steps of his started again, and I could see it, the lion in him, muscle and power coiled within him, his movements, the intensity of his gaze as he came towards me, eyes burning molten gold.

He stopped a few inches from me, making me tilt my

chin up to stay locked in his gaze as he towered above me. The vibrations from his purr penetrated my chest, rolling through me like a physical touch.

"Are you alright, Daff? Prowl?"

"Yeah," I croaked back to whichever guard had spoken. "We're good. You can go."

There was a moment of quiet, followed by footsteps and the door thunking shut.

"You okay, big guy?"

He still looked like he was coiled tight, waiting.

My fingers ached to touch him, to make contact with the heat of his skin.

Was that what he was waiting for?

"Can I touch you?"

"Please," his rough voice answered.

My fingertips grazed his stomach, making the ridges of hard muscle beneath them clench. They slid along velvet covered skin until my arms wrapped around him, my cheek resting on the dusting of hair covering his chest.

But he still hadn't reached for me.

"You can touch me," I whispered

His chest jerked beneath me, making me smile as I was enveloped in his warmth. He buried his nose in my hair, inhaling me deep into his lungs.

Which had me struggling to hold back tears. Because it really, truly hit me that Prowl had never been hugged before.

Or held anyone.

Let alone a willing female.

And I was willing. For maybe too many things between us.

Nothing had ever felt this good, this safe, this comfortable before. And if that's how I felt, how much more must he be feeling right now?

Was he becoming as attached to me as I was to him?

His huge, rough palm found my cheek, his crooked finger slipping beneath my chin, gently guiding my face up to his.

His thick brows furrowed, mashing together as his fingers traced the dampness under my eyes.

"You're sad. For me?"

"Just overwhelmed by the moment."

He rested his forehead on mine, one arm still holding me close, the other stroking my cheek.

"What do you want to do now?"

"Stay like this," his gruff voice answered.

I huffed a laugh, tilting my head just enough to meet his eyes without losing his touch. "I think we'd both end up with sore necks pretty quick."

"Worth it."

"Totally," I whispered back.

Which is how I saw him fully smile for the first time.

God, he was gorgeous. Wild, and so utterly different, with his deep set eyes, broad nose and angled jawline, but still beautiful in his own way.

I nuzzled further into his touch. "How about a nap? We can lay on an actual bed this time, and you can keep holding me without us both cramping up from the height difference."

His hold on me tightened, then I was flung into the air and into his arms, Prowl eating up the space between us and my bed in three long strides.

He managed to get us both on it and comfortable without breaking contact between us.

And I was absolutely okay with that.

CHAPTER 12
PROWL

The buzzer had my arms tightening around Daff and cracking an eyelid to see who came through. We'd had three safety checks through the night, each one requiring a verbal answer from both of us.

Daff's growl was as cute as the cubs. "Why can't they let us sleep?"

Between the steel I had pressed against her soft ass and my need to remember every second of this heaven, sleep had been the last thing I'd wanted.

She wriggled, her scent changing with her arousal.

Jeans voice froze her. "Daff, are you safe?"

I hid my grin in her hair at her groan.

"Yeah, Jean, I'm good."

"Prowl?"

I lifted my head to look at him. Jean stood just in front of Lara, Doc Paula and the vet.

Just as Jean took lead on the health and welfare of the on-base females, Lara was the on-base boss of ours. Three doctors ran the hospital along with half a dozen nurses, but I'd been specifically assigned to Doc Paula, unlike the others who saw whoever was available at the time.

Then there was the asshole vet. We'd been told he had a PhD in Zoology, alongside a psychology degree. Having those two together had the top dogs believing he was a necessary asset to The Compound, when in reality he was an over-applauded wanker who always thought he knew best.

"Still good, Jean."

Daff patted my arm. "Let me up, big guy. I need to pee so I can think straight enough to talk."

It was terrifying releasing her; but I refused to do anything that might break her trust in me.

Even if what she was asking for felt like a step towards death.

"Just gotta pee," she announced, heading for the toilet. "Feel free to start without me."

I watched her until she pulled the curtain across.

Lara took a half step towards me, drawing most, but not all my attention. "How are you feeling with all of us in your space?"

I swung my legs over the side of the bed, ignoring my hard-on as I stood, keeping my movements small and slow so I didn't alarm anyone.

I took my time looking over each one of them, scenting the air before settling on Lara.

The females were a nonissue. I felt a flicker of annoyance at having other males close to Daff, but they weren't a threat to her.

"Stable."

Lara's smile was genuine. "That's great to hear, Prowl. If things continue as they are? We're feeling extremely optimistic for you."

Daff's footsteps stopped beside me, her fingers slipping between mine as Doc Paula ran through her usual list of questions before approaching me for bloods.

Daff's wince told me when she'd slid the needle in and started the draw. My skin was so thick, and I'd had so many done, the pinch didn't even register.

"We'll have a second bed brought in by the end of the day," Lara said, looking at Daff. "We hadn't considered Prowl's reticence to continue sleeping on his side of the room."

"That won't be necessary," Daff said, her body going rigid beside mine. "We're fine with the sleeping arrangements."

She looked up at me, a small wrinkle above her nose. "Unless you want one?"

"I want what you want."

She hesitated, like she wanted to say something, but stopped herself, her attention going back to Lara. "We're good."

"I'm concerned with the level of co-dependency developing between them."

Thank fuck Daff's grip went from gentle to fierce in a heartbeat because it cut off my snarl just in time, forcing out a purr for her instead.

"And you are?" Daff asked, sounding pissed.

I fought a smirk at the vet's ruffled feathers over being asked.

"Doctor Lucus Helliot. Doctor of Philosophy in Zoology and clinical psychologist," he said, just like he had the other day. Only this time she got his list of titles tacked on the end.

"Not sure if you got the memo, *Doctor*, but Prowl's not a fucking animal."

"He was created in a lab with both human and animal DNA. We must consider all aspects of both to see to their appropriate management. Which is why I'm the leading consultant on their care."

"Are you serious?" Her head swung to Jean and Lara. "Is

he where you got the shitty advice to tell the hybrids never to expect females to ever want them?"

God, this woman. She was practically vibrating with anger for me. For all of us. And he wasn't even close to the top of the biggest asshole list of doctors we'd dealt with.

I pushed my purr louder for her, and Jean dipped his chin in my direction, acknowledging my effort.

Which was appreciated.

"While I agree we need to be mindful of them developing an unhealthy level of co-dependency," Doc Paula said, continuing the original conversation, "I think our ultimate priority should be Prowl's health, and doing everything we can to enable him to return to a fully functioning life outside these walls. All other concerns, excluding safety, should be secondary to this."

"Paula—"

She raised an eyebrow at him. "Do you have an issue with exposure therapy, its use, or documented results, Lucus?"

"If we can avoid it from the start—"

"At the expense of slowing or altering Prowl's potential for a full recovery?"

The asshole's jaw clenched. "If my opinion wasn't needed, I wouldn't have a job. And in my opinion, they're already exhibiting alarming signs of co-dependency that could be detrimental to all the hybrid's mental health and expectations. If they—"

"Enough!" Lara snapped, cutting him off. "I appreciate both your opinions, but the end decision is mine. While it's definitely something to be mindful of, I'm going with Doc Paula on this one. For now," she said, stopping the asshole before he could wind himself up for another round.

"What happens now?" Daff asked.

Lara gave me her full attention. "What would you like to happen, Prowl?"

Daff squeezed my hand, as if she'd felt the spread of warmth roll through my chest at Lara's question. At someone, anyone, letting me have a say in what my life would look like next.

I cleared the emotion from my throat. "I'd like to see my brother again."

For him to see me without bars between us.

"I think that's an excellent idea."

"If he handles it well, send in another hybrid," said the vet. "If he's already excessively attached to Daff, he could easily destabilise or attack. The full level of his protective instincts won't be triggered around us, and likely not King or Rage either, since they're part of his coalition."

Doc Paula nodded. "I agree with that plan."

"Jean?" Lara asked

"I'm on board as long as the current protocols continue."

"Daff? Prowl? Are you two okay with that plan?"

Daff looked at me.

"I'm good."

Daff nodded. "Me too." She looked back at me, her teeth tugging on her bottom lip. "And maybe Mandy? If she's feeling brave?"

I smiled back at her. "Absolutely."

"Let's see how the other two visits go before I clear her coming in."

"Thanks, Jean."

Jean nodded as his hand slipped to his belt, unhooking his pager. "I need to see to this. Is that everything?"

"I'd like a blood sample from Daff to compare to her pre-arrival take."

"Daff?" Jean asked, catching her shudder.

"Yeah, sure. That's fine," she replied, though she sounded far from it.

"I'll contact King and let him know you'd like a visit," Lara said, as Doc Paula tightened the strap around Daff's upper arm and swabbed her inner elbow with an antiseptic wipe.

Daff turned her head, pressing her face into my arm. Her skin had paled, and her breaths were falling shorter and faster. I turned towards her, careful not to jostle her as I stepped closer, my purr filling the small space between us.

"All done," Doc Paula said, releasing the cord from around Daff's arm.

"You'll hear from King soon," Lara reassured me.

"Thank you."

Lara nodded, and they saw themselves out, Doctor asshole shooting us both a frown right before the door closed behind him.

"Are you okay?"

Her head nodded against my chest. "I hate needles. Not that I should be complaining to you about them."

I buried my nose in her hair, her sweet scent rolling through me. "I'm sorry."

She squinted up at me. "What for?"

"This. Me. Doc Paula wanting your blood."

"You," she said, her palm settling against my cheek, "have nothing to be sorry for. I've said yes to every single thing that has landed me here in this moment with you, and I wouldn't change a single thing."

My hand found hers, holding it steady as I pressed my lips to her palm.

"See, that right there? The way you touch me? The way you look at me? Sometimes I wish..."

I gripped her hand as it tried to slip from me.

"Tell me. What do you wish?"

Her eyes fluttered closed. "I wish I knew if it was really me you wanted or if you'd be looking this way at anyone who was able to finally calm you."

My growl ripped through me, my fingers diving into her hair, forcing her head back and her eyes to fly open.

"You. Are. Mine."

"Prowl—"

"You get that shit out of your head right fucking now. You didn't just calm me. You saved my fucking soul. You stole my fucking heart. From the moment you stepped into my cage, you saw me. Me. And I saw you. You are kind and fierce and so fucking brave. If this, right here, is all I ever have of you—"

Her lips crashed against mine, shutting me up in the best possible way.

Her tongue slipped between my lips, drawing a shudder from me. I lost myself in her taste, in the feel of her smooth tongue grazed against the rough texture of mine.

Her hard nipples brushed my chest, her soft stomach pinning my dick between us.

She broke our kiss, dropping her head to rest against me, her short, panting breaths tickling the hairs on my chest.

CHAPTER 13
DAFF

If his words hadn't convinced me he meant it, that kiss sure as hell did.

Even now, he held me like a lifeline, his chest shuddering beneath me, his cock, long and hard, pulsing between us.

Probably aching with the same frustration as my clit, and the emptiness within me begging to be filled.

I didn't have a ton of experience in that department. Two jobs and a dependant dad had kept those interactions brief and noncommittal.

But I knew enough to know this level of need, of aching desperation, wasn't my normal.

"You sure you haven't done that before?"

His fingers, still pressing into my scalp, slid free, the gentle tug raising goosebumps across my skin.

"Never expected to."

He was gazing down at me with an intensity I felt in my bones.

"I'm here now."

"Thank fuck."

I huffed a laugh as I stepped back, instantly hating the separation, the immediate lack of his warmth.

It hadn't even been a week, and I was in so freaking deep with him. Where would we be another week from now? Another month? Two years was a long time, but looking at him, wanting him, craving him as I did, I knew it'd pass in a heartbeat.

When my contract was up, I'd have to leave him.

The thought of it, of this, of us ending, pumped ice through my veins.

What would happen to him when I left?

Would he fall apart again? Lose himself, wasting away until he died? Or could I help him enough to be able to leave him whole?

He'd been that way once; surely, he could find his way there again.

We'd fight our way there together, then I'd step back. Further and further, until he was completely fine and didn't need me anymore.

I wanted that for him. So freaking fiercely my chest hurt.

I'd leave him whole while my heart slowly shattered, piece by piece, with every step backwards, widening the distance between us until he could function without me. Until my contract was up, and they flew me out of here, leaving him behind.

He was so damn right when he said I was his.

I'd never been anyone's before. Never wanted to be. Too much time, too much energy.

But I'd never felt this way about anyone before, either.

The need to comfort. The need to protect. Which was laughable, considering what he'd been created for.

And yet, I'd never felt safer.

I had his back, and he had mine.

It wasn't something I was familiar with. Dad loved me, loved all of his kids, but we took care of him.

And Mum? Mum did until she didn't.

I needed to make sure he'd be fine without me. That I wouldn't leave him aching and lonely when I left. Not doubting his self-worth or his ability to be loved and accepted. Not doubting his humanity or his right to exist in the world he was forced into.

I'd leave him happy and whole, with his brothers by his side.

Even if it meant I'd leave broken, my heart and body forever haunted by his memory.

"You okay, Angel?"

"Yeah, big guy. I'm good."

"Promise?"

I swallowed against the thickening in my throat, the slight burn in my nose, the moisture at the edges of my eyes.

"Promise."

Because I was.

And I would be.

I'd just have to figure out a way to be, once he was no longer mine.

CHAPTER 14
DAFF

Both guards entered, positioning themselves on either side of the door, guns drawn but not aimed. King followed, only slightly hesitating before stepping past them.

Was he as nervous about this as I was? I darted a look at Prowl, standing beside me. His face was calm, his shoulders loose, his fingers tangled with mine firm but not clenched.

Two steps towards us, Prowl tensed. On the fourth, he twisted, a warning growl escaping as he shielded me.

Both guns rose, and King froze, his eyes flicking between us.

My heart thumped as I reached for him, my hand sliding up his back, resting on a slab of hard muscle.

"I'm good, big guy. King's here for you, not me. I'm not going anywhere."

The tension left his body, ebbing away with his next few breaths.

"Brother."

Prowl's head dropped then he strode forward, eliminating their distance and gripping King in a fierce hug.

Prowl cleared his throat, and King's eyes looked glassy when they separated.

"We're good," King said to the guards.

The guns were holstered, and the door closed behind them, leaving the three of us alone. Prowl pulled out a dining chair.

"When Lara said you were out—"

"It's good to be on this side of the room," Prowl said, pulling me onto his lap and wrapping an arm around my waist.

I leaned back against him and patted his arm, reassuring him I was staying put.

King hesitated, taking us in before sliding a book across the table and taking the other chair.

"It's not smut, but it's still a romance. When word got out about it, the library was flooded with requests. I managed to get hold of this one before they were all checked out."

"Did they have many?" Prowl asked.

"Not enough, and there'll be a wait before they can get more to us."

"What about ebooks? If you guys can access porn, surely you could access those, too?"

"We've only seen the clips that have been stored on the server for educational purposes,"

I snorted. "Seriously? Educational purposes?"

"Everything is done via satellite, with no access to the internet. And we don't have personal devices."

"So, you need hard copies. Did you read that one?"

"Yes," he said, his thick brows falling into a frown. "Is it an accurate representation of a romantic relationship? Of what a woman would like when in one?"

I glanced at the book. It had a cartoon couple on the front, the both of them gazing at each other—her in a flowery dress and him in a cowboy hat and boots.

"I'd have to read it to tell you."

It didn't have skulls, guns or handcuffs on the cover, so it looked somewhat promising. The last thing any of them needed was tips from a dark romance.

"There's been lots of questions. Lots of disbelief. And anger," he said, eyes flicking between us.

"Because of the books?"

"We had no idea monster romance existed. That women would be interested in it, or potentially us because of it. Even if it's just out of curiosity." He focused on Prowl. "Word has also spread about Daff. How she's not afraid of you, that she instigated touch and felt safe enough to sleep beside you, while comforting you."

Prowl kissed my head, his arm tightening around me.

Which just infuriated me more.

Who the hell wouldn't want Prowl? Or any of them, if he and King were any indicators of what the rest of the hybrids were like.

"It makes me so freaking mad that you've been given zero expectation of ever having physical contact, let alone sex or a genuine relationship. What's the point in bringing us here, of exposing you to us, if it was never going to be on the cards for you? To tease you? Test your resolve?"

"That's the consensus behind everyone's anger," King Said. "That they'd tell us we deserve the same freedoms and experiences as every other human, but also tell us to hold no hope of having what every other male has a right or desire to."

"Have they given you a reason?"

"All they've said is they didn't want to give us false hope."

"That's such a bullshit excuse. What's the bet it was the asshole animal doctor that pushed this?"

"Lara seems genuinely upset by the pushback." King leaned back on the couch, a sigh escaping him. "This is new for everyone. It's expected mistakes will be made along the way. In light of the new unrest, Sarge has called a meeting. It would be good if you could be there. The wolves are particularly restless, and another calm voice would be helpful."

"Sarge? He's the other hybrid they're sending to visit us, yeah?"

"Yes," Prowl answered, his breath tickling my ear. "Is he still our representative?"

King nodded. "He wants to nut out our biggest concerns and upsets and present them to Lara so we can address them quickly and efficiently."

"When?"

"Thursday."

I patted Prowl's arm. "If we keep progressing as fast as we have, and things go well with Sarge's visit, three days should be doable."

King's face looked wistful for a moment, his gaze brushing over every place Prowl and I touched. "I don't doubt it."

"How's Rage?"

King's shoulders fell. "He's claimed a home in the Wild Zone but won't tolerate anyone except me within its vicinity. And it's just that, tolerating. He barely speaks and runs almost completely on instinct."

"I'd like to see him."

"I'd like that too. I think it would be good for him."

The buzzer sounded as he stood. A guard entered and Kara followed, pushing our lunch through the door on her trolley.

King froze, the only sign of movement, the slow expansion of his chest stretching his black T-shirt even tighter with his inhale. His frown returned with his exhale, shaking off whatever had gripped his attention.

"I'll leave you to your lunch. I'm glad to see you happy, brother. I hope things go well with Sarge."

King gave Kara a wide berth, but she still froze as he passed, her eyes glued to the floor.

"He won't hurt you."

Kara's eyes flashed up to mine, widening slightly at my full-body contact with Prowl before dropping back to her cart, her movements jerky as she transferred our food to the table.

"I know." She hurried to the short bench top next to the sink, grabbing our breakfast plates and making them rattle as she dumped them on her trolley and fled out the door.

"I thought it was just you she was scared of. But she responded the same way to King. Do all the other women act like that around you?"

"I don't know. I was already here when the first group arrived."

I shook my head. "All she's doing is reinforcing the belief that you're too different or unsafe to be wanted."

"You're changing that."

Prowl pulled my lunch to me.

I stared at the stacked sandwiches. "I know. But it shouldn't have taken this long for that to happen."

"What matters is that they listen. For that, we need to clearly voice our issues and outline a plan to address them that Lara can sign off on."

"That's what Sarge's meeting is for?"

"That and to remind them to keep their shit together while we figure this out." He leaned back in his chair, drumming his fingers beside his plate.

"I think it would be good for them to meet you. To see how comfortable you are with me." He glanced up, his gold eyes flashing. "You'll be safe, I promise."

"I'm more worried about them being okay with me being there. It's a hybrid-only meeting."

"We're a package deal. If they want me there, they'll accept you being there with me."

"And seeing us together won't upset them more?"

"Possibly," he said, picking up the first of his three sandwiches. "But I think they'll benefit from seeing us for themselves and hearing your thoughts straight from you. So far, they've only heard things through the grapevine. And your insight as a female on their suggestion changes, and ways Sarge could present them to Lara could better help them understand things from multiple perspectives and ultimately streamline the process."

"Okay."

He took a bite before pointing to mine. "You need to eat."

"I'm not hungry."

"Did I do something?"

I reached up, my thumb soothing the wrinkled skin between his brows. "No. I promise I'd tell you if you did."

"Okay."

"I'm going to shower, then I'll see how I feel about eating."

His eyes heated, his wide nostrils flaring.

I should've asked if he'd be okay with just my voice this time. He'd survived my quick rinse yesterday without watching, thanks to King's company.

There were no walls or bars separating us this time if he panicked. And after the kiss we'd shared, ending up wet and naked in his arms, as he reassured himself I hadn't disappeared, wasn't a place I could trust myself.

Not after watching him touch himself.

And definitely not with the spark of heat already licking my insides at the thought of how hard he'd be watching me again. My thighs clenched against the growing ache as I took two steps back and turned, my hands finding the hem of my shirt and pulling it off.

Prowl had already lived a lifetime of shitty experiences.

I loved the thought of adding a good one for him—of adding a million and one good ones. Ones he could keep and remember long after I left.

My bra followed my shirt, then I leaned forward, tugging off my tights and underwear in one go, pausing just long enough to give him a full, bare view.

Thank God for waxing. Because screw the cellulite and stretch marks, and everything else the world said wasn't perfect about me. Feeling his eyes on me, hearing his harsh intake of breath, knowing how goddamn hard he would be for me right now if I were to run my hand down the front of him, tracing the lines of his abs all the way down...

My nipples went hard at the sound he made, more growl than purr.

I pulled the shower curtain open, sliding it as far as it would go before flipping on the water and turning to face him.

Prowl was watching me, eyes hooded with lust, his forgotten lunch sitting between white fingertips, gripping the edge of the table.

I checked the water temperature, then stepped beneath it, letting its heat penetrate my skin before reaching for a hand towel and soaping it up.

I started at the dip by my collar bone, watching his golden eyes follow my movements like his life depended on it, up the sides of my neck and back down between the valley of my breasts, slowly circling each one, the brush of slick cotton teasing my nipples into tight, hard buds.

His low groan followed my next dip, down my stomach

and each thigh, drawing back up again on the inside of each, so damn close to where I ached the most.

My eyes fluttered closed as I dropped the cloth, trading it for hands I wished were his.

"Eyes on me, Daff."

I peeled them open to find him standing just out of reach, his hand gripping his hard cock through the front of his sweats.

"You're so fucking beautiful."

His rough voice whispered over my exposed skin, raising goosebumps.

"Touch yourself for me. I want to see you come."

I whimpered at his request, the aching emptiness inside me demanding to be filled. Demanding I see him too, that we do this together.

"Only if you come with me."

His harsh breath answered as he slid his hand below his waistband and yanked it down, exposing two heavy balls and a cock begging to be rode.

He palmed the liquid on his broad head before sliding down a wide shaft with spirals of short, nubbed spikes.

Spikes that would no doubt feel like the tip of my nose if I pushed on the tip of it.

"Fuck."

My finger found my clit, the ones on either side spreading my lips to better expose it, as my other hand cupped my breast, squeezing it before creeping higher to pinch my nipple, a quiet moan escaping me.

"Daff."

I focused back on his cock, matching my tight circles to each of his strokes and keeping the biting pressure on my nipple.

"You're a fucking goddess, Daff."

My hips arched at the compliment, the building pressure within me starting to peak.

"I'm close, Prowl. So close. I want your cum on me."

It was the next best option if it couldn't be inside me.

He stepped forward and groaned, his free hand landing over my shoulder, his forehead pressing against mine, the only place we touched.

"Come for me, Angel. I need to hear what you sound like. Need to hear my name on your lips when you come."

My hips thrust forward again, my breasts arching with the movement, my nipples grazing the hair on his chest.

"Prowl..."

His forearm moved faster, his hand twisting each time it reached his head.

My body went rigid, locking in place as my orgasm hit, gripping me harder than I expected.

""Prowwwwwl!"

I floated down from my high, just in time to feel a stream of hot spurts hit my stomach, the falling water washing it away as quickly as it appeared.

A shudder ran through him as he released his cock for the back of my neck, his lips a whisper away from mine.

"Angel ..."

"Kiss me."

Prowl pressed his body to mine as he devoured me, his lips and tongue making love to me like our bodies would have.

Desperately. Fiercely. And with a shit ton of worshipping.

We only stopped because of the cooling water.

He shut it off and reached for my towel, wrapping it around me.

"Daff—"

"We're good," I said, cutting him off with a too-brief kiss. "I'm good. I promise."

He hesitated, his watchful gaze searching my face. "No regrets?"

"No regrets."

Except for the niggling curiosity of how his cock would feel, dragging along my insides as he thrust inside me, how his balls would feel slapping against my ass each time he bottomed out.

Next time.

And there'd be a next time, I was sure of it.

CHAPTER 15
DAFF

"Mandy!"

The blonde bombshell barely hesitated before entering our room. I'd never been the hugging type, but it felt like everything else had shifted on its axis since coming here, so I leant into the one she offered, so damn grateful that it'd been her that sat next to me when our group waited at the terminal.

She pulled back to give me a thorough once-over.

"Are you still safe and happy in here?"

She didn't know me well enough to notice the heat in my cheeks, and I didn't know her well enough to know if she'd tell me off or high-five me for the orgasms we'd shared yesterday or the constant body contact we'd maintained since.

One thing was for sure—Prowl was definitely making up for his lifetime of no physical contact.

"I am."

I stepped to the side so she could see Prowl in all his bare-chested glory. He'd put the romance book down and swung his legs off the side of our bed but stayed seated.

"This is Prowl. Prowl, meet Mandy."

He nodded but stayed put. It took me a moment to realise he wasn't being rude; he was staying still and quiet so he didn't spook her.

"Hi," she said, her eyes running over him. "Are you okay with me visiting for a bit?"

"If Daff's happy, I'm happy."

Her eyebrows popped up. "Well, that's a bit sweet. And not what I was expecting."

"What are the other hybrids you've met been like?" I asked, pointing to the couch under the dark window and plopping down beside her.

"I've only got close and personal with the cubs so far. They're so freaking adorable."

"How are they?" Prowl asked, surprising me.

"Happy, for the most part. And so dang smart." She looked back at me. "We do mostly play-based learning, but they pick up everything we show them way quicker than expected. And their agility and speed is mind-blowing. They're obsessed with obstacle courses at the moment, and the way they move through them..." The wonder on her face was so genuine I wanted to hug her.

Who knew what those cubs had been exposed to and put through before being freed?

"Are any of them struggling?"

Mandy hesitated, earning a low rumble from Prowl and an answering flinch from her.

I grabbed her hand. "It's okay. He won't lash out or go crazy. Will you, Prowl?"

His rumble turned into a purr.

"I'm sorry. I just need to know they're okay. I haven't seen them in a long time, and I worry they've felt abandoned by me."

Mandy instantly softened.

"They know you've been unwell and doing your best to

get better so you can see them again. There are two cubs that seem to struggle the most. King visits most days, and those are the days they do their best."

Prowl nodded. "They were always more settled when we were there. I think it soothes their family instinct to feel like a complete pride."

"I thought prides only had one male, but you and King get along fine. At least from what I've seen," I said, looking at him. "Is that because of your human DNA?"

Mandy leaned forward a little. "How are things when you and your brothers are together? It doesn't cause tension or fights between you?"

"Male lions are occasionally known to form coalitions. Usually between brothers and up to three at a time. That coalition would then lead and protect the pride."

"Is that what you, King and Rage are?"

"King and I were always together. Rage would come and go, but he was always welcome with us."

"I've been wondering," Mandy said, her eyes flicking to me before focusing on Prowl, "how Rage would interact with the cubs. If it would speak to his instincts and find their presence soothing. I can't help but think that if he's running on instinct, it could ultimately prove beneficial. Lions aren't meant to be on their own."

She sat back, waving a hand in the air like she was physically dispersing her voiced thoughts. "Anyway. I know it's a moot point, and the higher-ups would never allow it. I just couldn't help wondering if the calm King brings to the cubs would work in reverse for Rage."

"I appreciate you thinking of my brother."

He looked so sad saying it; I had to force my butt to remain on the couch next to Mandy instead of crossing the space between us and hugging him.

"How do you think you'd go visiting them?" I asked instead.

"My next goal?"

"Why not? You've been fine with the guards, the med check team, King and now Mandy. If things go well with Sarge, it's a reasonable ask. Especially since you see them as family."

"Then that's what I'll ask for."

"What we'll ask for."

His lips tipped up.

"You have a fierce friend, Mandy. I'm glad she's on my side."

"She's brave, I'll give her that. And there's no denying how much you've changed. Just think. Another few weeks doing this well, and you could both be out of here, doing your own thing again."

My stomach twisted, and Prowl tensed.

She was right. A few more weeks like this, and this thing, this connection between us, could be over and done.

Was his reaction excited at the thought of getting out of here or distressed over us being separated?

Mandy's gaze landed on the book in Prowl's hand.

"How did you get a hold of that? Every single romance book has been checked out, and there's a waiting list a mile long."

"That would be my fault. When word got out that some of us liked to read smut, particularly paranormal and Sci-Fi smut, the hybrids went a little rabid in their attempt to get hold of some."

"Why?"

"Because some idiot zoologist convinced them no normal, rational female would ever want to be intimately involved with them because of their split species' DNA, tortured pasts and unique genital traits. And when they heard that there was, in fact, a whole demographic out there that would be turned on instead of horrified by those differences, hope made them desperate to read it for themselves."

"God, that's awful. Did you all really believe no woman would ever want you?"

Prowl nodded, his golden eyes finding mine.

"Daff disabused the med team of that notion."

"And explains the hybrid anatomy lesson we all got."

My thighs clenched at the memory of what Prowl's said anatomy looked like, and this time, Mandy noticed my spreading blush.

"Tip of your nose, hey?"

"I couldn't tell you," I said after clearing my throat.

I ignored her answering huff of disbelief.

I hadn't lied. I didn't know what his spikes felt like.

So far, I'd only seen them.

"The good news is, we've been told the library has ordered a bunch more, so you won't be waiting forever to get one."

"Uh-huh."

The buzzer sounded, startling a jump out of Mandy.

"Dang, that's loud."

One of the revolving guards stepped in, followed by the second, positioning themselves on both sides of the door.

"Sarge is here."

Prowl placed his book beside him and rose to his feet, keeping his movements slow. I was up and beside him without a second thought.

If he was going to hurt someone, it'd be Sarge, not me, and only if I couldn't keep him calm.

Mandy was on her feet now, too, looking nervous.

"You should leave," the second guard said, motioning for her to head for the door.

"We'll be fine," I reassured her. "They're just doing their job, making sure everyone is safe each time Prowl tries something new."

She nodded despite still looking unsure.

Which was fair enough since both men had their weapons drawn and aimed at the floor near Prowl's and, subsequently, my feet.

"Good luck with your visit. I hope you get to see the cubs soon."

"Me too," Prowl said, his eyes on the open doorway, his nostrils flaring slightly.

"Thanks, Mandy."

She nodded and was gone.

"Ready?" the first guard asked.

I slipped my hand into Prowl's, lacing our fingers.

"Send him in."

Sarge stepped into view, stopping in the doorway.

He was not what I expected.

A fine, grey fuzz coated his skin, appearing thinner on his face and hands. It thickened and grew long at his hairline, which sat fairly far back on a forehead. The ridges above his brown eyes were almost severe in the way they protruded, as was his wide jaw.

Definitely a gorilla.

He wore a black tank, stretched over a huge barrel chest, exposing arms thicker than Prowl's thighs, and cargo pants encasing legs even wider.

He was an absolute mountain of a hybrid and slightly terrifying to look at until I noticed the tiniest twitch by his hairline.

It was the cutest, daintiest looking, fuzz-covered ears I'd ever seen.

Which seemed to change him from terrifying to adorable in the space of two heartbeats.

"Prowl."

Warm brown eyes met mine.

"I'm Daff."

Prowl's grip tightened.

Sarge nodded. "It's nice to put a face to the name I've heard so much about."

Prowl's low growl filled the room, and I spun to him, pulling his face down to mine with my free hand.

"He's just saying hello."

His eyes dropped to mine as he leaned forward, inhaling against my skin.

"I'm yours, and I'm not going anywhere. And you really want to see the cubs, remember? We've got this."

His pressed a kiss to my forehead, there and gone again, his warning cutting off as he straightened.

"It's good to see you, Sarge. I appreciate you coming." Prowl settled on a dining chair, pulling me onto his lap, his arm securely around my waist.

Marking his territory, like he'd done with King.

Sarge moved as carefully as Prowl usually did, barely hesitating before turning his back to us and taking a seat.

"You can leave," he said, dismissing the guards.

Surprise rolled through me at the authority in his voice and again when the officers holstered their pieces and stepped out.

When I looked back at the enormous hybrid, he was studying us with an intensity that sent a flutter of nerves through me.

Prowl's purr, so low and soft it was barely more than a vibration travelling through his chest to my back, relaxed me enough to sink back against him.

A slight twitch of Sarge's fingers, hanging loosely over his spread knees, was the only sign he felt anything at the sight of Prowl wrapped around me and me being totally okay with it.

"Do you mind if I ask you both a few questions?"

I looked at Prowl, who raised an eyebrow at me.

"We'd be happy to," I answered, loving that prowl had left the decision up to me.

Sarge nodded, looking thoughtful.

"Everything we've heard has been filtered through at least one other person. I trust King and value his word, but I struggled to believe everything he said."

"You guys have been dealt a crap hand and given even crappier advice on what to expect going forward, especially regarding relationships, both physical and emotional."

"We're aware of that now, thanks to you. Though not all of us are ready to believe or hope for it just yet."

"Do you think seeing how we are with each other will help or make things worse?"

"Both, to be honest. Which is why I'd like you at the meeting. I didn't think it possible when King suggested it, but now that I've seen you for myself?"

"We'll be there," Prowl said, the breath from his words tickling the fine hairs on the back of my neck.

"If you're okay with me being there too," I quickly added.

If Sarge was the official hybrid representative, the last thing we needed was to step on his toes.

"Of course." His eyes flicked over my shoulder. "Be prepared for some unrest. It won't be aimed at either of you, but it's best you're aware and prepared for it. Especially if your grip on this is fragile," he said, motioning between us.

"We'll be fine," I cut in, before Prowl could respond or take offence. "As long as I'm safe, there shouldn't be an issue. My safety is the only thing that seems to bother him."

"Understandable. I'll make it clear no one is to approach you without being invited first."

"Thank you."

His eyes roamed the room, taking in the closed bars of Prowl's former door and the one bed on this side of it.

"The contact between you. Is it because touch is the most effective, because you're both curious or because you have feelings for each other?"

I braced myself for Prowl's response.

His arm tightened, but he didn't roar or rage at the question. Lions peed to mark their territory, right? Because he didn't do that either, thank god.

"She's mine."

Sarge's curious gaze flashed to me.

"And he's mine."

"Even though you both know Daff's contract has an end date?"

"We'll deal with it then."

I nodded, since I couldn't seem to push aside the emotion clogging my throat. Because I was totally screwed. There was no way I was leaving here with my heart intact.

Prowl seemed so sure, so confident, that we'd deal with it when it happened. But he hadn't ever witnessed heartbreak before. How someone could turn into a shell of themself, only breathing and eating because it was expected of you, and it was the minimum requirement to keep your body alive and functioning.

Sure, Dad had been physically broken by his accident. But emotionally? Mentally? That didn't happen until after Mum left us in her rearview mirror.

Maybe Prowl would be fine, though. He'd survived forms of anguish and grief I could never fully understand. And he'd have his brothers, the cubs and the other hybrids who could support him through it.

Me? My NDA meant I couldn't tell a soul. That my grief,

my broken heart, would be my own burden. Mine, and mine alone.

Prowl's purr started again, notching up a level in intensity. Sarge took it as his cue to leave.

"I hope you can make the meeting. There'll be a lot of questions, and I'd appreciate your thoughts, both of yours, on what we discuss. I'm genuinely glad to see you well again, Prowl. As awful as it's been for you, it will prove to be that catalyst we needed to bring Daff here and give us bigger, better dreams for ourselves and our future."

His hands found his pockets as his eyes roamed over us one last time.

Whatever he was thinking made him nod again, before knocking on the door to be let out.

CHAPTER 16
PROWL

Daff's hand squeezed mine.

Her attempt at reassurance was sweet but unnecessary. She'd filled the deepest cracks in my soul, sealed them closed with her embedded inside.

She was a part of me now. My sanity. My peace. My home. My heart's sole purpose now was to keep beating for her.

Because I wouldn't survive losing her.

"Are you ready?" She asked.

Lara, the guards and whoever else stood waiting outside for us to emerge were braced for me to lose my shit. To be overwhelmed by the onslaught of scents and react violently.

I knew I wouldn't.

My instincts had claimed the anchor they'd needed. My lion had needed a purpose. A family. He'd needed his mate and had recognised her in Daff. Others might question my theory, but every warped cell in my body knew it to be true.

So no, I wasn't worried about leaving our quarters the way everyone else here was.

My restlessness, my concern, was about keeping Daff safe.

The need to protect her was what had me in a heightened state. And with no way to prepare, to know exactly who or how many were waiting for us? I was gritting my teeth, holding back a growl that would have us hustling back into that room and behind that goddamn door.

Admittedly, I'd happily stay locked in there forever, just the two of us. But Daff deserved better than spending her days trapped in there with me. What if she started feeling claustrophobic and needed more space? Or wanted to go outside, and I couldn't follow?

Someone could hurt her or try to claim her. Take her as their own, so she never came back.

"Look at me, big guy."

She was facing me, one hand on my chest, the other on my jaw.

"Deep breaths. You've got this. I know you do."

I gripped her tiny wrist, basking in the softness of her skin as I kissed her palm.

Her lips curved into a smile.

"Think of those cubs waiting for you. How happy they'll be to see you."

"I'm fine, Angel. As long as you're safe, I'll be fine."

Her face softened. "Nothing's going to happen to me."

Yeah, because I sure as shit wasn't going to let it.

"Ready?" Henry asked.

I nodded, not looking away from her.

"Yep," Daff answered, moving to my side.

"Jean, Lara, Doc Lucus, King and two more officers are waiting outside. The immediate area has been temporarily cleared."

The bands around my chest eased with the information. "Noted."

"They'd prefer you exit separately. Daff first, you second. We'll cover your back."

My growl erupted before I could think to stop it. Now was not the time to be putting everyone on edge.

Were they still not convinced that I'd gladly kill myself before I'd ever hurt her?

"We go together. Physical contact works best for us," Daff said, jaw set in defiance.

"What are your orders?" I asked, forcing myself to look away from her.

He was human, in full tactical gear, with The Compound's standard two guns strapped to his belt. The larger of the two, a Taser that would kill anything but us, was drawn and aimed at the floor. His shoulders were braced, but his hands were steady, the radio strapped to his shoulder silent.

They were all good things. It meant there'd been no last-minute changes and that he was alert, but not feeling trigger-happy.

"First and second have a shoot-to-kill order. We have incapacitate. If you remain stable through the meet and greet, we'll escort you to the cubs. First and second will remain outside, third and fourth will follow you in. All four will accompany you on your return."

"The meet and greet?"

"Ready. They'll wait for you to approach."

"Okay. You ready, Angel?"

"As ready as I'll ever be. You?"

"Ditto."

She sucked in a loud breath as the officer beside her spoke into his radio.

"Prowl's ready to exit."

"Confirmed. Area is still clear, opening the door now."

I tightened my grip on Daff's hand, keeping my eyes trained forward despite the urge to look at her, knowing she was watching me.

The outer door swung open. Early afternoon light spilled onto the floor, the rush of fresh air bringing with it an onslaught of scents.

Males. Human and hybrid. Lara. Soil. Decomposing leaves. Floral notes.

"Ready when you are, Prowl."

Two steps, three blinks, and I was outside, adjusting to the sunlight.

Jean, Lara, King, and the vet stood dead ahead, the guards on either side braced with guns drawn but aimed low. The rest of the area was cleared as promised, though I could hear voices floating from not too far away.

The urge to yank Daff to my chest and shield her with my body ran feral, the need pulsing through my veins with each heartbeat.

Rationally, I knew King, my only genuine threat, wouldn't take her from me. No one here would except maybe the jerk-off.

Just the thought of that bastard taking her away, touching her, breathing the same air as her, had rage choking my lungs.

"Breathe, big guy."

I inhaled on her command. Breathed in her scent and enough rational thought to cut that line of thought. Doc Paula had already weighed in on that, and Lara had the final call. I had to trust in that—in them—to get through these next few minutes, just long enough for the bastard to watch me emerge and leave without incident.

I stepped in his direction.

CHAPTER 17
DAFF

If I didn't need every ounce of my attention on Prowl, I'd have turned my face up to the sun and basked in its glorious warmth, soaking into my skin.

Who knew you could miss something so mundane, so incredibly much?

Prowl's movements were smooth and loose, but I could feel the tension in him through our joined hands.

Could they sense it, too?

Nobody was watching me, which was fair enough. Jean wore a frown, his fingers giving the occasional twitch, like he was ready to pull one of the guns strapped to his belt. Lara looked hopeful and a little proud. Like a mama bear believing in her cub. And Doctor Helliot?

The bastard looked like he had a bad taste in his mouth.

He really needed a dick punch.

We were halfway there when Doctor Helliot started forward. A roar ripped from Prowl's throat, the deadly sound raining goosebumps as he cut me off, manoeuvring me behind him and keeping me there with his forearm, pressing me to his back.

"Shoot him!" Helliot yelled.

"No!"

"Freeze!"

Prowl's roar rang louder.

"Don't shoot him! I'm fine! He's protecting me!"

"He's too reactive! Take him down and remove her!" Helliot yelled over the top of me.

"Everyone hold!" Lara's voice cut through, loud and clear. "Daff, are you okay?"

"I'm fine! Prowl's protecting me, not hurting me."

"What are you protecting her from, Prowl?"

I'd pressed my hand to his back, rubbing slow circles in the small space between our bodies.

His voice was rough and low. "Helliot."

The prick had the audacity to look insulted. "He's seeing threats where there are none. He's proven he's not stable."

"You provoked him by coming towards us!"

"I did no such thing."

"We were told you would wait for our approach. You changed the plan!"

"If he can't handle the unexpected, he shouldn't be allowed out."

Prowl was still braced in front of me, his body a rigid wall of protective muscle, waiting for the volley of words between us to stop.

I slipped my arms around him, plastering myself against him, hugging him from behind.

"She's right, Lucus. You started forward when the plan was to wait." This, from Jean.

"Again. If he can't handle unexpected—"

"Enough! Prowl, I apologise," Lara said, cutting Helliot off. "Doctor Helliot shouldn't have moved towards you. You have my word that both you and Daff are safe."

"She stays with me."

"As long as it's her choice to stay, no one will take her from you."

"Agreed," Jean said after her.

"My choice is to stay with you," I said, squeezing his waist. "Always. So, we're good, big guy. Let's get this done so we can see the cubs."

He slowly straightened, his hands finding my arms, still locked around his waist. I pressed a quick kiss to his spine and stepped to his side, letting my arms fall and our fingers tangle.

I watched him lock eyes with each of them before squeezing my hand and starting forward again.

He stopped in front of King.

"It's good to see you outside, brother."

Prowl took another step and embraced him with his free arm, propelling me forward with the other.

King blinked back obvious emotion when they separated, his eyes settling on me with his nod. "Little sister."

Dang it. Now it was me blinking back tears, because coming from him, that endearment hit all the feels.

He was acknowledging me as family. His family.

I had a pretty strong suspicion that counted as a hell of a lot when coming from a hybrid. "Hi, King."

Prowl turned to the others. "Jean. Lara."

He ignored Lucus.

"How're you feeling?" Lara asked.

Prowl hesitated, seeming to take stock of his body and our surroundings.

"I'm good. Heightened awareness." He squeezed my hand. "Otherwise, I'm unbothered by the extra noise and scents.

"I'm happy to hear that. Do you need to retreat, or are you feeling up to visiting the cubs?"

His shoulders dropped, relaxing with the offer.

"I'd love to see them."

King slapped his shoulder, his air of seriousness dropping with his smile. "They'll be thrilled to see you."

"Do they know we're coming?"

"We didn't want to disappoint them, so it will be a surprise."

Prowl nodded, the insinuation clear.

"If everyone's ready?" Lara asked.

Nods answered her.

"We'll walk to the care centre. That way, you can stretch your legs and see how you handle the increase in scents and noise." She tilted her head towards the four officers. "Your guards will take a diamond formation around you both. They'll keep your path clear and stop any approaches before you're ready to deal with them. We'll follow behind you."

"Sounds good," I said, squeezing Prowl's hand.

The way to the care centre was paved, with low gardens on one side and a road on the other. Two golf buggies passed us, a few hybrids waved, while others stopped, their eyes finding and staying on our linked hands.

Proof that there were females out there happy and willing to touch them.

Prowl's thumb brushed mine, the repetitive motion accompanying his low purr.

Damn that man. Hybrid.

I should be focused on soothing him, not the other way around.

A ten-foot-high fence opened with King's thumb. The two extra guards remained on the footpath while the rest of us entered, only opening the glass door that was covered in small, painted handprints once the outside gate had closed.

Mandy greeted us, bouncing on her toes at the sight of us.

"You're here! The cubs are waiting on the carpeted area for—"

"Prowl!"

"It's Prowl!"

"Proooooowl!"

His name in a dozen high-pitched voices cut her off, making her grin wider.

Three steps, and we rounded a corner into a large, carpeted area. Prowl fell to his knees, his hand sliding from mine just in time to catch a swarm of little girls barreling into him.

A million questions peppered him, battling for first place amid coos of adoration and not-so-subtle demands that he never, ever, stay away that long, ever again.

He shuffled them forward, herding them into the middle of the room before settling on his backside and encouraging them to sit with him. It only took a little coaxing to sit, but instead of finding a spot in front of him, they settled on him, the few missing out on direct contact, squishing in as close as they could.

His purr filled the room, drawing happy sighs and even a few higher-pitched purrs in response.

It was so freaking adorable, my ovaries hurt.

My giant hybrid was the centre of a snuggle pile made of small, ridiculously cute, squished-nose cubs. Prowl looked up from them, his smile blinding.

It was that moment, that exact moment, I knew I was in love with him.

"Have you ever seen anything so hot in your life?" Mandy asked.

I snorted as I side-eyed her. "I got dibs the moment he responded to me."

She waved her hand. "Doesn't mean I can't appreciate the view."

"It's heartwarming, isn't it?" Lara said, startling me and Mandy

"Absolutely," Mandy answered, smirking at me before giving her attention back to Lara. "They're only ever this happy when King is here."

"As human as they are, the need for their pride supersedes everything else."

"Even Immy and Lulu are happy."

Lara nodded. "Those two worry me the most." She pointed to the two cubs with arms wrapped around Prowl's neck, taking up the most physical space against him.

"All the cubs have issues, but Immy and Lu struggle the most. Anxiety, symptoms of depression, restlessness. King's had it hard, splitting his time between Prowl and the cubs.

"Without regular contact, the cubs start declining in mood and energy levels. Immy and Lulu are affected the most and can rapidly spiral. But time with their big brothers always has them bouncing back to their brightest."

"Did Rage ever interact with the cubs?" Mandy asked.

Lara's raised eyebrows in Mandy's direction. "No. The cubs were fragile when they were rescued, physically and mentally, and we've never felt him stable enough to expose them to him."

"But if he's lost to his instincts, those instincts would theoretically drive him to keep the cubs safe. His need to care and protect would override everything else."

"Theoretically, yes. But—"

"And if the cubs are soothed by King and Prowl, isn't there a decent chance that the cubs could soothe him in return? And potentially, if his instincts are soothed enough to not overwhelm him, his rational, human side might have more of a chance to operate, helping him to function in a much more normal capacity."

Holy smokes. Did Mandy hear how passionate she sounded right now?

"I'm impressed. You've thought a lot about this."

Mandy shrugged, a blush, the lightest of pinks, staining her cheeks. "I've spent a lot of time with people who face physical and mental challenges. Many are overlooked and never given the chance to reach their full potential because those who can help them haven't, or worse, won't dedicate the time and patience needed.

"I guess I just see so much potential for Rage, with so many untried avenues. And after everything Rage and all the hybrids have been through, I want to help any way I can."

"It's admirable. And no doubt one of the reasons you made it here. But as much as I'd love to help Rage and the potential I see in your suggestions, we ultimately can't risk the safety of the cubs."

Mandy's shoulders fell. "I understand. I do. I'd never want any harm to come to them."

All three of us looked at the cubs, still draped over a grinning Prowl.

He lifted his chin in my direction.

"I think you're being summoned."

"What? Why?"

"You're about to find out," Mandy said, her hand on my back nudging me forward.

I crossed the space between us with what felt like hundreds of wide, little brown eyes following me.

"Ladies, this is Daff. She's mine," he said, grabbing my hand and pulling me down beside them.

Somehow, all those little eyes widened.

"Did she teach you how to purr?"

"She did."

Three blonde heads leaned towards me, sniffing.

"She kinda smells like you."

His smile widened.

"That's because he's always touching me," I whispered.

"That's because he likes hugs. Don't you, Prowl?"

"Absolutely. And Daff's hugs are the best."

"Really?

"Are you sure?"

"Even better than King's?"

"Even better than King's," he answered, shooting a smirk at the other lion, who was holding the wall up with his shoulder.

One of them scooted over to me on her knees. "Do you like hugs?"

"I like Prowl's hugs."

"And Kings?"

"I haven't hugged King yet, so I don't know."

"And she never will," he said, shooting me a look that made me roll my eyes.

"Do you like hugs from cubs?"

I tapped my chin, pretending to think about it, though my insides were melting at their cuteness.

"You know, I haven't tried cub hugs before. Do you think you could give me one so I could know for sure?"

The little girl side-eyed Prowl. "Is she allowed to hug cubs?"

"I suppose I can share some of Daff's hugs with you."

She squealed as she leapt into my arms, wriggling until she was smooshed against my chest, her nose pressed into my neck, arms looped around me.

She inhaled against my skin, then snuggled closer.

"You smell nice."

"Thank you, sweetheart. You smell nice, too."

"Prowl was right. You do give nice hugs."

Another three bodies appeared, all vying for space on my lap.

"Hey! Those are meant for me!" King said, joining us with a smile on his face. Another two left Prowl to leap up into his arms. He pulled them close before smirking at Prowl. "Unlike you, I need to get them wherever I can,"

"Puh-lease. The whole group of women I arrived with are into... those same specific books I like," I said, trying to make my words cub friendly. "They'd be crazy not to jump on you."

His eyes focused behind us, his smile dimming. "We'll see."

Right. That wasn't awkward or a little bit sad at all.

"Alright cubs, time to let them up!" Mandy said, clapping her hands for attention. "Head outside, and we'll have another go at this morning's obstacle course."

The cubs moaned and groaned and they dragged their cute bodies off us and filed outside; the pouting faces and sad waves ditched for shrieks and laughter the moment the sunlight hit their skin.

"I'll see you guys later," Mandy said, waving before heading out after them.

Prowl stood and offered me his hand, keeping hold of it once we were up.

I smiled up at him. "That went well."

"Really well."

Lara joined our small bubble of happy. "I know you're keen to attend the hybrid meeting tomorrow. Sarge has asked you be there, with an invitation extended to Daff. I feel confident you're capable of attending. Jean?"

He studied both our faces. "Prowl's made it clear his primary concern is keeping Daff safe. I'm happy to clear Daff to attend."

I braced myself for whatever the idiot doctor had to say. Except... his opinion never came. "Where's Doctor Helliot?"

"He didn't come in."

Rightio then. Lucky us.

We followed Lara and Jean back outside, as Jean laid out my security plan for attending the hybrid meeting.

"Two officers will escort you to and from the meeting. King and Drill will take point on safety once you're inside." He looked at Prowl "At the first hint of unrest, I want Daff out of there, whether that unrest is from you or any other hybrid."

"Absolutely."

"Of course," King echoed.

"Great. With that sorted, Jean and I will head off." She pointed to the gate ahead of us, where only two of the four guards remained. "The other two have been dismissed, so it's just the four of you and King, if he wants, heading back."

Lara looked between the three of us. "Good luck tomorrow. I hope... I hope you all figure out what you need to feel seen and heard. I'll do whatever I can to help implement it."

"Thank you," King said, his voice a touch rougher than normal.

I don't know how the higher-ups could do such an amazing job finding Lara as a champion for the hybrids, and so utterly craptastic with employing Doctor Helliot.

Jean offered his hand to Prowl, the action surprising me. Prowl shook it, a nod passing between them.

Had Jean just given Prowl his approval?

CHAPTER 18
DAFF

Light and noise spilled onto the concrete ahead of us, a layered mix of low male voices punctured by the occasional ring of laughter.

King and a mammoth of a hybrid, similar looking to Sarge, with a high, wide forehead, boulders for shoulders and a fine, velvet fuzz, the colour of storm clouds covering his skin, waited just outside the open door.

Our guards slowed behind us. King acknowledged them with a nod.

"You must be Drill," I said, craning my neck to meet his chocolate eyes.

He blinked like he couldn't quite believe I was talking to him.

I squeezed Prowl's hand, both to warn and reassure him, before offering my other one to Drill.

"I'm Daff."

He did another slow blink, his attention falling to my waiting hand.

Sympathy flooded me over his uncertainty. Was it nerves from never touching a female before? Or was he a little slow on the uptake? An all brawn and no brains situation?

Either way, I felt for him.

He looked to Prowl for direction. Or was it permission? Which made me bristle.

"You shake it," I said, maybe a touch too forcefully.

My tone pulled his attention back to me, where he still hesitated before slowly creeping his hand forward. It felt like forever before it finally reached mine. His hand completely engulfed mine, while at the same time barely touching it.

I grinned up at him. "Nice to meet you, Drill."

"You too."

His soft voice startled me, but he was too busy dropping my hand like I was a hot coal to notice.

"You're the last to arrive. They're waiting for you."

King turned, and we followed him in, Drill falling in behind us. Two steps in, silence choked the indoor basketball court as sixty-odd pairs of eyes devoured us and the places we touched. Chairs squeaked and shuffled as we headed up a clear path that led to Sarge, standing front and centre of the gathering.

Two chairs sat slightly behind and to the right of him.

Drill positioned himself behind them and faced forward, his arms folding over his enormous chest.

Prowl took a seat in the plastic chair, then pulled me onto his lap, his arm wrapping around my waist, almost making me roll my eyes.

It seemed his standard go-to position when other hybrids were around.

Sharp, staggered inhales and muttered four-letter words followed his move.

I wriggled back against his chest, sinking into him. The sea of hybrids, of blatant, intense stares, kicking up my heart rate.

The loneliness, the fragile hope, and varying levels of disbelief levelled at us were heartbreaking.

I wanted to find Doctor Asshole Helliot and wring his fucking neck for all the things he'd let these males believe about themselves. There was a line between implementing safety protocols and damaging their sense of self-worth, and he'd crapped all over both.

It upset me even more that Lara and Jean hadn't picked up on it themselves.

King sat beside us just as Sarge started speaking.

"As you can see, the rumours are true. Prowl has a female who freely and willingly touches him and accepts his touch in return. King and I have both witnessed it and now you all have to."

"I do more than accept it."

Prowl's arms tightened around me in response, but I mustn't have muttered it quietly enough because two dozen heads swivelled in our direction.

"We want to hear it from her!" someone called, which was followed by a wave of nods.

Sarge looked at us. At me.

"Yeah, of course." I went to stand, but Prowl's arms turned into iron bands, locking me in place.

I patted his arm. "Let me up, big guy. They need to hear this."

"You can do it from here."

I shot him a dirty look over my shoulder. "Really? Short of lifting your leg and peeing on me, I think it's pretty clear to everyone I'm yours."

Prowl shrugged.

Well then. It looked like I was talking to them all like this. I raised my hand, giving them an awkward wave.

"Hi everyone, I'm Daff. Sorry if you can't see me down

the back. This guy won't let me stand up, so I'll have to do this from his lap."

A few heads halfway down lifted, and a handful down the very back stood.

"Right. I don't know how much you've heard, so I'll give a quick rundown what's happened and my thoughts on it, and then maybe we can do some Q and A?"

Sarge nodded, and Prowl kissed my temple, setting off another round of whispers and oaths.

"I arrived with the women in group B. I didn't have time to get the full brief on things here, just enough to know that you're hybrids who were rescued, and this is your new home. Lara and Jean cut our intro short because of things going south with Prowl. I was the fourth person to see him, and obviously, he responded to me. He's been improving in leaps and bounds since.

"We had nothing but time, which meant we got to learn about each other. This was when I was clued onto the fucked up expectations they'd given you regarding women, relationships and sex. And to be clear, they are fucked up."

The noise level rose until Sarge raised his hands, holding them up until the room fell quiet.

A hand went up, but I was too short to see who it belonged to.

"Blade?" Sarge said.

"Is it true you touched him first?"

"I did, yes."

"Why?"

I looked to Prowl, unsure how much information about him he was okay with me sharing.

"I was having a nightmare," he said, surprising me. "And it upset her. She tried soothing me with her voice and getting her scent close to me. When I didn't respond to either of them, she touched me. She stayed there and slept beside me."

Four letter words echoed around us, followed by half a dozen more raised hands.

"I heard she brushed your hair."

"She did."

"It was awkward doing it through the bars, but we managed."

"Why did you do it?" someone else called out.

"Because it was a mess, and I wanted to help him."

"I've got hair you can brush."

Prowl shoved me behind him, his growl thundering around us. "Daff's mine!"

"Shit!" .

"Prowl! Stand down!" Sarge commanded

I shoved past Drill, who'd mirrored King's move to intercept him. The huge hybrid flinched away from me, making it easy to face Prowl.

His feet were spread, muscles coiled, teeth bared.

Double shit.

"Look at me, big guy, I'm right here. All yours. No one's taking me from you."

My trembling fingers had buried themselves in his beard, grazing his skin, feeling his warmth as I willed him to look down at me.

"I need you to look at me Prowl, please. Please look at me."

He gave nothing away, no hint that he'd heard me.

"Please, Prowl."

His eyes, the only part of him that moved, lowered to me.

"You're mine, and I'm yours. Ignore the jackass. He's jealous, that's all. They all know I'm yours."

His arms came around me, burying his nose in my neck as he squashed me against him.

"Thank god. I thought I'd lost you."

"Mine," he rumbled, after another deep inhale.

"I know. And now there's no question that they do, too."

"Is he okay?"

I turned my head, just far enough to see Sarge and the two officers hovering in the doorway behind him.

"We're fine. Aren't we big guy?"

Another slow inhale, then he pressed his forehead to mine. "Yeah."

After a fleeting kiss to my nose, he straightened to his full height, staring daggers at the hybrids behind me. He gave me just enough room to turn back around and settle back on him, his arms rigid bands around me, the muscles in his thighs still coiled with tension.

The male who'd said it—a hybrid wolf with a lean body and jaw that protruded far enough to almost look like a muzzle, was still staring at me, his gaze a little too intense.

A lot of eyes were.

I started rubbing Prowl's forearm, the only place I could reach to soothe him and, to be completely honest, myself too. The last thing we needed was a setback, not when he'd been doing so well.

King and Drill retook their places, and Sarge cleared his throat, drawing everyone's attention. "Let's discuss the books."

I blew out a breath, grateful for the redirection.

"Daff?"

I nodded. "Smut is the classy term used for romance books with sex scenes. Unlike porn, the story is all about the couple falling in love and getting their happily ever after. There's a particular fan base of women who love reading alien, shifter, and monster smut.

"These generally feature a human female with a male of a different, intelligent species and their differently equipped cocks. There's enough of an interest in the sub-genre that adult stores carry a variety of alternative dick-shaped dildos to fit with the fantasy of being done by the main male character in their book.

"I can confirm the library has bulk-ordered various romance books at our request. If you are one of the few who were able to get hold of one, please return it as soon as you're done, so those on the waiting list aren't stuck there for long."

"Is it true the women in your group all like monster smut?"

"Yeah, but that doesn't mean they're all going to want a relationship or to jump into bed with you. Some might, the possibility is absolutely there, just... be mindful.

"Some women have no problem hopping into bed with zero expectations of anything more between you. Still, others can be really reserved with that kind of thing, or need an emotional connection, or a solid relationship first.

"I think the biggest take from this is, the reasons they've given you, your past, your DNA, your different junk; there's a ton of people out there who would still wholeheartedly want you exactly as you are.

"You guys deserve the same opportunity and expectation of sex, love and meaningful relationships as every other person on this planet."

"You see us as monsters?" The voice came from a dark-furred feline in the back. He looked similar to Prowl, with high cheekbones and a wide, flat nose, but he was dark everywhere Prowl was light, his black hair short and slicked back, his eyes a startling emerald green.

"Hell no!" Prowl lifted with me, letting me up while

keeping hold of me. "Your physical differences do not, now or ever, make you monsters."

My gaze drifted across them, their differences stark but not terrifying. They settled on the feline who'd spoken.

"There will be assholes. People who will hate you for your differences or want you because of them. But there are intolerant people and kink chasers everywhere, and they've been around long before your arrival. Someone having an issue with any of your differences is a reflection of them, not you. Never let anyone, even the higher-ups, tell you otherwise."

"Which brings us to why we're here and what we want going forward," Sarge said.

"The rules need to be changed," someone said.

Heads nodded.

"I need specific, actionable requests."

"We should be allowed to approach the women when we want to."

"And touch them."

"We should be allowed in their zone."

"They should be allowed in ours!"

"Have them make a list of women open to dating us."

"And fucking us!"

"Enough!" Sarge called over the converging voices. "We're not going to be able to change everything, not at first."

A rumble followed that statement.

"It's easy to say what things we want changed, but we need to provide them with specific alternatives that won't interfere with the women's safety or feelings of it."

"Can I make a few suggestions?" I asked.

Sarge raised an eyebrow, and the sea of heads facing me nodded, willing to listen.

I cleared my throat, shoving my second thoughts aside.

"What Sarge said about us feeling safe is right. They're not going to allow any changes that mess with that. Like coming into our zone. That would freak most of us out, wondering who was out there and if someone was going to break down our door to get to us."

I winced at the responding calls of anger.

"Let me clarify! Please! I don't know how exposed you've been to the outside world, but there are hundreds of years of history of women being knocked around, and our homes and beds invaded by uninvited, unwanted men.

"That worry is a fact of life for us, wherever we live, not a specific worry about you as hybrids. Maybe what we need is a neutral living zone, where those who want to, can live in a shared space where everyone can come and go as they please?"

The slowing nodding heads gave me courage.

"I also think you should be allowed to approach anyone you want, as long as their request to be left alone is honoured—and that should go both ways, for everyone. As for a list of interested women?"

I bit my lip, thinking. "What if there was a sign or symbol used instead? Like a ribbon or a badge that could be worn, both you and us, for whoever was open to the possibility of dating or sex."

More nodding. Including Sarge. "I like those ideas." He studied the gathered hybrids. "There's a lot more to be considered, but we need a starting place, and I like these suggestions. I invite you to have a think on those presented, and pass your thoughts on to your representatives before 10 a.m. tomorrow."

He looked at us. "Thank you, Daff, for your thoughts, for accepting one of us, and for giving us hope for a future we hadn't thought possible."

Ooof, that made my heart hurt. Especially since I didn't

feel like I'd done all that much besides call out the shitty expectations they'd been given.

"If you'd like to leave first, we'll give you a few minutes before following you out."

Prowl nodded, ran his eyes over the sitting hybrids, dipped his chin, then propelled us out, his arm wrapped around me, gluing me to his side.

I had just enough time to wave before Drill's giant form following behind us blocked them from view.

Prowl stopped at the edge of the pavement. "Thank you."

"For what?"

His eyes held me as solidly as his arms, his fingers stroking my cheek. "For once again, giving us hope."

My stomach twisted, and I fought the urge to bury myself in his chest. Did he not realise that there was nothing I wouldn't do for him? I was completely and utterly in love with him. A terrifying thought when we could only end in heartbreak.

I had a contract with an end date and a heart that would likely never heal.

I gripped his wrist and turned my head, kissing his palm.

He deserved to be loved. To feel worthy. To have every hope and opportunity that came his way. So I'd give him everything and love him enough over the next two years to fill two lifetimes and pray it didn't kill me when I left.

CHAPTER 19
PROWL

T he wind chasing leaves past us was on the cool side, but Daff and Mandy wore jeans and hoodies, and Sarge, Drill, King and I ran too hot to feel anything but content.

I kissed Daff's temple, then took another bite of my sandwich, grateful for the invitation to eat with them, and the guard keeping his distance.

Unlike most bases, ours had been designed with a pointed focus on integrating nature with the structures we needed to make it a viable home.

The best thing about it was the park at the base's centre. They'd left the larger trees intact, surrounding them with manicured gardens, jogging paths, and a handful of picnic tables.

All circling a spring-fed dam.

"How did the meeting go last night?"

Sarge paused with his steak sandwich halfway to his mouth.

Did all these women have steel balls under their sweetness? Daff was braver than anyone expected, but Mandy was holding her own just fine.

She popped a sauce-covered chip in her mouth, ignoring the hell out of Drill's stare.

The gorilla wasn't even trying not to.

Drill grunted, finally drawing her attention, but he'd looked away from her, frowning at the three of us.

Trying to figure out which one of us had kicked him under the table.

Sarge ignored him. "Daff had some great ideas that we're keen to see implemented."

Daff wiggled beside me. "You are?"

"It was a solid yes on all of them."

"Do you mind me asking what they are? Since they'll affect me if they're approved."

Sarge settled his food back on his plate. "Relaxing the initial contact rules while honouring a person's right to decline. A symbol to wear, signifying openness to a relationship and a shared living area. We also want investigations done on our ability to have children. Despite our conflict with undergoing further studies, the consensus is, these ones are worth it."

Surprise had me straightening, and Daff's hand gripping my thigh.

A child willingly conceived in love wasn't something I'd ever contemplated. Would I have one if I were able to?

My hand slid over Daff's, my heart a heavy thud in my chest, watching her bury her teeth into her bottom lip. She looked up at my gentle squeeze, her dark eyes searching mine.

She'd talked about studying and buying a house. Did she want kids and a family too? I could see her, lips curved with joy, her small hands rubbing slow, soothing circles over the large swell of her stomach, my larger ones following their path.

Could she see it, too?

"Wow," Mandy said, blinking rapidly.

"Is that a good wow or a bad wow?" Daff asked her, breaking our connection.

"Good. Mostly." She popped another chip into her mouth, chewing it slowly.

She had both Sarge's and Drill's full attention.

"What don't you like about them?" Sarge asked, leaning forward on the table.

Mandy swallowed before answering. "The symbol thing's great, and I can see a future need for the shared living area, especially as couples emerge. And you should definitely know if kids will ever be on the cards for you."

"But?"

Her left shoulder lifted and dropped. "But I like knowing I'll be left alone unless I want to interact with someone. The thought of potentially getting mobbed every time I'm in a shared space is a little worrying."

Sarge folded his arms as he leant back. "So, we should continue being treated like animals to be avoided, or a lesser class of people, forever waiting for your permission to approach?

"Do you know that if one of you were to fall or faint and we caught you, we'd still face an investigation that would decide whether the instigated touch was necessary and what our consequences would be for it?"

"What the hell?" Daff whispered.

Mandy's face paled. "You're absolutely right. You should be allowed to approach anyone you want, any time you want, and you shouldn't need permission to touch someone, especially if it's what they need in that moment."

"I like to think the current rules are there to help us interact in a way that makes you feel safe," Sarge said, his face mashing with a frown.

"But now you can't help but wonder if those rules are

also there to prevent relationships from developing?" Daff asked.

Drill dropped his massive head. Sarge gripped his shoulder, squeezing it.

"It's getting harder not to think that way."

Daff nodded. "I'll give you one guess whose agenda that would've been."

"I don't understand," Mandy said, looking between us all.

Daff turned to her side, resting against my arm as she gave her friend her full attention. "You know the zoologist slash shrink, Doctor Helliot?"

"I've seen him at the care centre, observing the cubs."

"While Lara makes the final call on all things hybrid related, his opinion carries a lot of weight."

"Why?"

"Because we're just as much our animal as we are human," I said, unsure if Daff would comfortable saying it. "And our instincts reflect that. They're right to factor in both sides in their decisions regarding us."

"So... what's the problem with him?"

"The *problem*," Daff answered, already sounding half pissed, "is he let the hybrids believe that while they're more than animals, they still aren't human. And if they aren't fully human, they shouldn't expect the same futures or rights."

"Maybe he's right, and we shouldn't have those things." Drill's voice was soft but firm, like he'd considered this all before, and reached the same conclusion.

Mandy's palms slapped the picnic table, making us all jerk. Everyone's heads snapped in her direction. "Don't you dare tell me those little girls I look after every day don't deserve love, family and everything else good this world has to offer!"

Drill's eyes widened, the poor male looking more than a little terrified by her outburst.

And maybe a little awed by it.

"Even animals have the right to bond and breed. Daff's right. No matter which way you look at it, your rights aren't being upheld. If he's representing your animal sides, he's failing."

"Maybe his issue isn't with you having those things, but having those things with us," Daff whispered. "Different can mix with different, but not different with normal."

"You think he'd have less of a problem with us getting attached if you were a female hybrid?" I asked.

"It makes sense, doesn't it? And it's not like it hasn't happened before, between colour, ethnicity and class."

Sarge still had a frown plastered across his face when he spoke. "It's a thought worth considering, especially as we move forward, pushing for change."

I nod my agreement, along with everyone else.

Except King.

"King? Are you okay?"

Warmth spreads through my chest at Daff's concern for him.

His foot gets a swift kick when he doesn't answer, his attention fixed over my shoulder - at Kara, drinking from a water bottle.

"Do you...like her?"

My brother doesn't hesitate before answering. "She doesn't like hybrids."

"Then why are you watching her?"

I may have been trapped behind glass, but I'd seen his reaction to her each time she came through the door, pushing her trolley.

He dragged his eyes away from her and levelled a hard stare at me. "I'm not."

Drill huffed. "Could have fooled me."

"I'm not," he said again, his focus going back over my shoulder.

My brother could swear it until he was blue in the face, but his obsession with her was obvious. He deserved to be happy, but I doubted he'd find that with Kara. Whether it was fear or disgust, she wanted nothing to do with us.

She was a dead end for him. I hope he realised it sooner rather than later.

Mandy pushed her disposable plate forward, making room for her elbows.

"How's Rage doing?"

King looked at her.

"Better, since he's settled in the Wild Zone. He's claimed a cabin and a small territory around it, which the others are respecting. I leave supplies with him every week when I visit. He tolerates my presence, which is good, but gets aggressive with anyone else who tries."

"I'd like to see him."

Daff squeezed my thigh. "Is that possible without me?"

"You're coming with me."

"But if he isn't coping with others—"

King shook his head. "You're female, human and zero threat to him. And it's clear you're Prowl's. That in itself, separates you from all others. He'll accept your presence; just don't expect a warm welcome."

"Okay."

"Do you think he'd be okay with any female in his area? Or is Daff only okay because she's Prowl's?"

King swallowed a mouthful of water before answering Mandy. "I don't know. We have a lot of questions regarding him and things that could potentially help him. But every single one carries a risk we haven't been willing or able to take."

Mandy's shoulders slumped. "That's the same answer I get to all my suggestions."

She stood, dusting off the back of her jeans and leaning over to give Daff a one-armed hug. "Sorry guys, but my breaks almost up. If I don't head back now, I'll be late getting back."

"Give those cubs an extra big cuddle from me," Daff called.

"Will do. We should do this again!" She said, shooting us all a smile.

A half wave, and she was gone, following one of the jogging paths out.

"She's nice."

I grinned at Drill. "Look who can talk again."

Daff elbowed me in the ribs, the sharp jab surprising me. "Leave him alone. He's allowed to be shy."

Drill dragged thick fingers through his dark hair. "I'm quiet, not shy."

"It's okay either way. Mandy's a knockout and would make most guys lose their tongues."

Had Daff looked in a mirror? I leaned down, close enough for her to feel my lips brush her ear. "She's not anywhere near as beautiful as you."

She looked up at me, a smile tugging at the edge of her lips as she raised an eyebrow. "I make you do a double take?"

"You do more than that."

She bit her bottom lip, keeping her eyebrow up as she slid her hand from my thigh to my cock. The warmth of her palm made me jerk beneath her touch, and the sweet scent of her arousal hit my nose.

She gripped me through my pants, and my vision blurred around the edges as I stood, lifting her with me.

The hard-on I could deal with, but the thought of anyone else smelling her need?

Hell fucking no.

"Prowl—"

"Thanks for lunch. We'll see Rage tomorrow," I called over my shoulder, already hustling Daff in the same direction Mandy had gone.

"Bye, guys!" She shot me a dirty look. "That was rude!"

"So is letting them smell your need for me. You're lucky you're not over my shoulder right now so I can get you home faster."

She was power-walking beside me, but it still wasn't fast enough.

She snorted. "The guard behind us would Tase your ass in a heartbeat."

"Which would delay my plans of licking every inch of you until I find the source of that scent."

"Fuck," she whispered, making herself go faster.

I grinned down at her. "You like the thought of that?"

"Who the hell wouldn't? Now shut up and let me focus on breathing so I don't embarrass myself with how unfit I sound hustling my butt for you."

I slapped said butt, drawing a playful glare from her and a few sets of shocked eyes. "You're perfect."

"Besides walking too slow."

She waved to the guard sitting next to our door, her body practically vibrating as she waited for the beep to sound and get inside our room.

She spun towards me, her hands landing on my chest as I cupped her face.

"You're the most beautiful thing I've ever seen, Angel."

"You're supposed to say that after you've got my clothes off."

My mouth landed on hers with a growl, her tongue as eager as mine.

A shudder ran through her, and she pulled back, chest heaving as she tugged my shirt.

"Off."

She peeled off her hoodie and I nodded at her jeans, repeating her demand.

"Off."

She grinned as she wriggled them off and kicked them aside.

"Better?"

It would be once she was naked.

She stepped towards our waiting bed. "You ready to pay up on that promise?"

I shook my head. "You still have too many clothes on to do a thorough job."

Another shudder ran through her as her hands went behind her, unhooking her bra.

I closed the distance, my tongue finding her small, hard nipple.

Her head dropped back with a moan. I gripped her ass, lifting her onto our bed, my tongue refusing to leave her skin.

Her nails dragged against my scalp as I traced the curves of her breast before falling onto the other, my cock hard and aching for her.

The bastard could wait. Because this? Touching her, tasting her? It was everything.

My hands found her hips, my fingertips catching on her G-string, tugging it down. She lifted, her hot cunt pressing against my abs as I slid the lace free.

Her breath shuddered as I settled between her legs, lifting them over my shoulders so I could fit where I so desperately needed to be.

My thumb slid down her wet slit first, parting her on its way back up, brushing her clit.

Her hips surged with my name, and I inhaled, closing my eyes as I drew her scent into my lungs and held it there, wishing I never had to breathe it out.

"Fuck, you're pretty," I whispered as I examined her, memorising what was mine.

I leant down, my nose dragging along her dampness until I couldn't stand it a moment more, and let my tongue take over.

She arched with another moan, her tangled fingers tugging my hair, her thighs locked behind my head.

My fingers slid inside her, curling upwards as I focused on the firm nub that had her bucking beneath me.

"Prowl!"

It was too fucking much. Her smell, her taste, the feel of her wet heat squeezing my fingers. I freed my cock and thrust against the mattress, keeping time with my fingers, sliding home inside her.

Her breaths were coming fast and shallow, her sweet voice escaping her in thready moans until she tensed beneath me, her grip on my hair threatening to dislodge me from where she needed me most.

Her muscles choked my fingers, and I thrust again, imagining them gripping my cock.

Her body eased beneath me, her muscles relaxing into a boneless state. I eased out my fingers and gentled the swipe of my tongue but didn't stop until she tugged on my hair again.

"Come here." She cupped my face in her hands when I reached her, studying my face before pulling me in for a kiss.

Her legs slid around my waist, her feet digging into my ass until my cock was trapped between us.

"Your turn."

"I don't need it, Angel. Seeing you come undone was enough."

"Would you try something with me?"

Was there anything I wouldn't do for her? "Always."

"Ditch your pants and crawl up behind me."

"Daff—"

"Just do it." Her bossiness earned her a chuckle, and my obedience. She rolled onto her side, and I crawled in behind her, sliding one arm beneath her neck, and the other around her waist, pulling her to my chest.

"I'm not completely sure how this'll go but..."

She lifted her leg and reached between them.

My heart thundered, my breath escaping me in a rush as she guided my cock forward, settling him between the folds of her pussy before lowering her leg again, trapping me there. Her fingers grazed my spikes, then added pressure to the underside of my cock, keeping me firmly against her.

"Rock your hips."

My lips found her shoulder, my empty hand her soft breast, as I drew my hips back then thrust forward.

A hiss escaped me at the sensation of my trapped cock sliding against her wet warmth, her ass pressed against me, eliminating the space between us.

"Again."

She felt too fucking good to deny.

"Keep going!"

Either my head or my spikes were hitting her clit, because her breathy moans started again; the sound of her finding pleasure from the feel of my cock driving me higher.

My lips parted, my teeth finding her skin, aching with the fiercest need to bite down. To mark her as forever mine and filling her until she dripped with my cum. My fingers found her nipple, clamping and rolling until she arched into my hand.

Her whimpered words drove my hips faster.

"I'm coming."

I followed her over the edge, my body jerking, my vision blurring, my cum covering her belly and the underside of her breasts.

I ran my nose along her neck, ignoring the burning in my jaw from refusing to mark her as I breathed her in. Peace filled me at the combination of our shared scent.

CHAPTER 20
DAFF

King stopped our golf cart before the access point into the Wild Zone. It was separated from the rest of the base by a three-story electric fence topped with razor wire and intermittent voltage warning signs. There was a single booth next to the gate, manned by a wolf hybrid.

King stepped out ahead of us. "Tracker."

The wolf lifted his chin, his eyes sliding over Prowl and landing on me.

"She has permission," King said, before he could ask.

He scented the air.

From the bits and pieces I'd heard about the other hybrids, their differences reached deeper than just their looks. Prowl said the wolves' ability to scent was enhanced to where it was rumoured one of them could detect the minute changes in a person's scent, enough to tell if they lied.

Which meant my brain had swung straight to how often people's BO must bother them, then how the heck they could filter out all the other scents bombarding them to detect that one singular change.

It was crazy to think about.

And an ability I could see a lot of powerful people wanting access to.

"Rage?" The Wolf asked.

King nodded.

"Do I need to remind you that most of them haven't met a female without bars between them?"

I leaned into Prowl's warmth.

"We've got her."

He handed King a huge ass Taser, then slid a key into the dash, turning it. The gate hummed and rolled open.

"Does he really need that?" I asked, jerking my head towards the Taser King was clipping to his belt.

"Protocol," King said, glancing back at me.

We entered a small enclosure, the gate behind us closing before the one before us opened.

"You okay, Angel?"

I licked my dry lips. "Yeah."

A soft purr rolled from his chest.

"How long will it take to reach him?"

"Walking? Twenty minutes," King said. "He doesn't leave his territory, so I know where to find him."

We followed King, stepping beneath a fairly solid canopy of trees, teaming with life. Bird calls. Humming insects. Branches flexing. Leaves whispering.

We were a few minutes in when I glimpsed a decent-sized building, hidden among the trees. "What's that?"

"That's the lodge. Most of the wolves split their time between the two sides of the island. That's where they stay when they're here."

"They don't have cabins like Rage?"

"Cabins are for permanent residents. There's only so many they can fit on this side, while maintaining a sense of separation from each other, so those that come and go either sleep outside or at the lodge."

King's back went rigid, and Prowl tensed.

My legs tried to lock, but Prowl tugged me forward, maintaining our pace.

"Prowl—"

"We're fine," he said, his eyes scoping and occasionally snagging on the surrounding trees. "Just a few males being curious."

"A few?"

"They're keeping their distance."

For now. But what if they approached?

A shudder ran down my spine, my hand turning clammy in Prowl's.

He'd promised time and again he'd keep me safe. But here in the Wild Zone, with no barriers and males who either couldn't or refused to live on the populated half of the base...

How many would be too many before he and King fell, protecting me?

I focused on my breathing, trying to ignore the tension in my shoulders and tightening bands around my chest as I watched my sneakers crunch over fallen leaves. King slowed to a stop with Prowl beside him, and me sandwiched in the middle.

Ahead, the not quite there path continued to a small building, not much bigger than my side of Prowl's containment area.

"Rage!" King yelled.

Something rustled to the left of us, making me flinch.

The two lions looked at each other, Prowl giving a small nod.

"We're coming to you!" King called.

They started forward, Prowl gently tugging me into motion.

Maybe I shouldn't have come. Or stayed on the other side of the fence with Tracker. Every day was a huge leap forward for Prowl. He absolutely could have managed this without me, especially with King by his side.

What if Rage took one look at me and hated my guts? It would devastate Prowl. Maybe enough to sever the strands between us, tying us together.

I swallowed against the lump in my throat, forcing my feet, trapped inside invisible cement blocks, to keep moving.

King knocked on Rage's door, but they both had their heads tilted to the left, listening.

Prowl released my hand, trading my fingers for my lower back. "He's coming."

Rage stepped from the shadows beside his cabin. He was bigger than King, his hands and feet more like elongated paws than palms, his skin more fur than the fuzz coating Prowl and King.

He was dark to their light, yellow to their gold, feral to their hard-earned tame. It radiated from him, sending a shiver rippling down my spine.

Prowl cleared the emotion from his throat. "It's good to see you, Rage."

Rage grunted, his body braced like he couldn't decide if he was about to bowl us over or run the other way.

"Daff, this is my brother, Rage. Rage, this is Daff. She's mine."

Prowls hand moved to my hip, Rage's eyes following the movement.

"Are you well?"

Another grunt.

"Should we go inside?" King asked, knowing it would help Prowl and I feel safer.

King headed to the door when Rage didn't answer, taking his silence as a yes. The door swung open on silent hinges, and King disappeared. Prowl gave my hip a squeeze and let go.

Right. In we go.

I filled my lungs, licked my dry lips, and nodded. I could do this. I absolutely could. It'd be a defendable space with no hybrids watching from the shadows.

How many lived on this half of the base that weren't wolves coming and going?

Prowl was talking to a still-silent Rage when I reached his door. I paused at the last moment, resting my hand on the doorframe.

King was inside, and Prowl would be right behind me. Feeling this nervous was beyond ridiculous. I had no reason to—

My hip and shoulder slammed into the hard ground, the air forced from my lungs, crushed beneath a massive weight.

My ears rang from multiple roars, black spots blinking in and out of existence.

Another Roar, louder and fiercer, pushed a whimper from my lips, barely uttered before the weight disappeared.

Air rushed into my lungs, and I rolled to my side, spikes of pain stabbing me with each hacking cough. I flinched at the hand on my shoulder.

"Daff, you okay?"

It was King touching me. That meant...

"Prowl..."

His fingers tensed, and I blinked past the damp, fuzzing my sight.

Flesh hit flesh; wet, loud smacks followed by another furious roar.

"Prowl! Take Daff and go. She needs you!"

My vision cleared enough to tell them apart. Prowl had

Rage on the ground, a hand tangled in his hair, yanking his head back, the other at his throat, blood dripping from a gash down his side.

"Give, Rage! Don't make me kill you!"

Fuck.

King rose to his feet. "Do it, Rage!"

Prowl shifted his weight, digging his knee harder into his lower back.

"Don't! Please don't." He'd never forgive himself for killing Rage. Not once it was done, and the heat of the moment gone.

Rage's head wrenched back further, forcing a pained grunt from him.

Still, he struggled, the claws of one hand buried in the soil, the other on Prowl's wrist.

"I will kill you, brother. Don't make me do it." His voice barely sounded human. "Rage!"

Anger rumbled from him, but his hand released Prowl's wrist.

Prowl shoved his face into the ground, leaning down with all his weight.

"If you ever touch her again, I will put you down." Prowl leapt off him and swung me into his arms, cradled me to his sweaty chest and fell into a sprint.

I hoped it was his sweat.

"I'm sorry."

He blinked, the only sign he'd heard me.

"Will he be okay?"

"King will see to him."

I pressed my forehead against him, closing my eyes as I breathed him in, willing the ache in my chest away as I rocked in his arms.

He'd fought his brother for me.

Pinned him down.

Threatened his life.

If I hadn't been there, it would never have happened.

This rift between them. The choice Prowl had been forced to make between keeping me safe and harming his brother.

"Tracker! Open the gates!"

Prowl squeezed through the first one before it finished opening.

"Faster, Tracker!"

"What happened?" The wolf asked.

"Rage happened. Call medical. Daff needs a doctor. I'm bringing her to them."

"And Rage?"

"King has him covered."

The gate behind us locked.

"He still alive?"

"Yes," Prowl answered, his voice void of emotion.

The fence separating us from Tracker started moving.

"Take the cart. I'll get another for King,"

"Call medical," Prowl repeated, ignoring the cart and sprinting past.

I looked up when he slowed. Two people stood in the glass doorway of the hospital, waiting for us. One set of eyes were on me, the other on Prowl.

"This way." The Doctor said, forcing Prowl to follow her at a slower pace. "What happened?"

"Rage charged her. Had her pinned beneath him."

"I'm okay."

He placed me on the edge of a hospital bed. "Left side impact. Possible concussion," He said, not acknowledging me.

"Prowl, please. I'm okay." I hurt, but I wasn't bleeding.

"And you?" The Doctor asked him.

"Don't worry about me. Take care of Daff."

"Ben will check her over while I see to your injuries."

A growl ripped through him, making the male nurse wince and me realise how silent he'd been since he'd picked me up.

He hadn't purred for me.

"You check her."

"Because he's male?"

"Because you're the doctor," he snarled back.

She pursed her lips but nodded.

"But you're bleeding!" I cried, reaching for him.

His eyes, glowing gold and so utterly feline, shot to me. "You first."

I closed my eyes but nodded. It was clear there'd be no persuading him.

The Doctor moved to my side. "Where are you hurt?"

"Left side, like Prowl said. My ribs hurt, and I hit the back of my head, but I don't think I have a concussion."

She flicked on a miniature torchlight. "Look straight ahead for me."

I blinked past the blinding light, searing my eyeballs.

"Pupils look good. Let me feel the back of your head."

Gloved fingers probed my scalp, making me wince.

"You have a small lump and no bleeding. No concussion, but you'll most likely have a decent headache. If you start feeling dizzy or nauseous, you'll need to come back."

"She will."

She moved to my ribs.

"Take a few deep breaths for me, and tell me where it hurts and what the pain feels like."

"It hurts everywhere as soon as I breathe in too deep."

She nodded, her gloved fingers pressing into them.

"Nowhere specific?"

"No."

Another nod. "You might show some bruising, but

nothing's broken. Lift your arm for me. Good. To the side. Above your head. Okay. Roll your shoulder for me. And forwards." She lifted my arm by my elbow, looking it over. "You'll have a few bruises, but it looks fine. Can I see your hip?" I lifted my shirt and lowered my leggings, exposing it.

She gave it a once over, then turned to Prowl. "No major damage. She just needs painkillers and rest. Watch out for increased dizziness or nausea. Patch through to me if anything else pops up, but she should be fine."

He nodded as I slipped off the bed.

"Up," she said, directing him to it. "Will you lay down?"

"No."

She nodded like she'd expected his answer. "Then sit on the end of it so I can get close enough to patch you up."

Prowl grimaced, but did it, his eyes on me as she changed her gloves. Then, she looked him over, without touching him.

"I need to clean a few grazes, and the cut down on your side needs stitches."

"I'll be fine."

"It's non-negotiable."

He grunted but didn't make another sound as she made her way around him, putting antiseptic wherever she saw blood.

She stepped back. "Daff, do me a favour and stand between his legs."

"Um..."

Did he even want me that close to him right now? Things felt... broken between us. The feeling could have absolutely been all in my head until the realisation he hadn't purred for me.

How could that not be a bad sign? Every other situation we'd been in, he'd started at the slightest hint of me feeling upset.

She raised an eyebrow.

"It will make this easier for him."

Shit. Of course, it would.

I stepped between his thighs, guilt strangling me. How much of his life had been spent in rooms similar to this? Stark white, medically sterile, the sounds and smells universal, whether the procedure was needed or forced on you. Like all of his would have been.

I gripped his thighs, meeting his eyes. "I'm sorry, Prowl. For all of it."

His hand found the back of my neck and pulled me forward, close enough to tuck me under his chin.

"Only a few stitches, since I know you heal fast and prefer not to have them."

Prowl nodded above me.

"Do you know what state you left Rage in?"

"King's seeing to him."

She hummed in response. "We can send in supplies if he needs them."

He grunted. "I'll tell King."

"All done," she said, removing her gloves with a snap that echoed around us. "Since you're keen to be out and about, I want you both to pop back in the morning for another once-over. It'll save Paula the trip in to see you."

"Any particular time?" I asked.

"Whenever you're up and ready."

"Thanks."

Henry was waiting outside with a golf cart.

"Are you here for us?" I asked, looking around.

"Jean sent me. He's caught up in meetings but wanted a visual check on you."

"Of course he did," I muttered. "Alright then. Let's go home."

Prowl helped me up, then followed me on with a smoothness that belied his injured side.

Two minutes and we were home, the two steel doors locking us back inside our bubble.

"Prowl—"

"I need you," he rasped, his hands finding my jaw and pulling me in for a searing kiss. "I thought I'd lost you."

The kisses kept coming, peppering my cheeks, lips and jaw. His teeth grazed my neck, and his frenzy stilled. "I need to mark you as mine."

"Do it."

I didn't care how he did it or if it would hurt. I needed to be his, with a desperation that obliterated everything else.

"Make me yours, Prowl. I need to be yours."

He kissed me hard, lips and teeth clashing as we tore off our clothes, his hands roving my body, sliding and squeezing until every inch of me blazed with need.

"I need you inside me."

He lifted me with a growl, his teeth grazing my nipple as he followed me onto our bed, his thighs pushing mine apart.

My head tipped back, my body arching beneath the rough lap of his tongue, paying homage to my clit, then plunging inside me.

The pressure was already building, but I pushed at his head, needing him to hear me.

"Your cock, Prowl, I need your cock. Please!"

The please got his attention.

"You're sure?"

"I need all of you."

My words made him shudder as he rose above me. His thick head dragged between my folds before pausing at my entrance, drawing a whimper from me.

"Angel..."

I wrapped my legs around him, nudging him closer, increasing the stretch.

"Fuck," he whispered, his body trembling above me.

"Don't stop," I whispered, my fingers finding my clit to help ease the way.

He knocked my fingers aside, replacing them with his thumb. The spark of pleasure had him sliding in a few more inches.

His hips started moving, the feel of his spines, the fullness of having him inside me, making my eyes roll.

"Eyes on me, Angel," he said right before he slid all the way home.

We both groaned at the sensation, acknowledging the moment. Another groan, and he began to move. Our bodies slicked, our tongues clashed, and my orgasm began to build.

"I'm gonna come."

His hips drove faster, his mouth falling to the place where my neck met my shoulder. My body locked, my orgasm peaking as fire pierced my skin, his bite driving me even higher.

Prowl shuddered above me, his hips jerking as he came.

It took him a moment for his teeth to release me, but I barely felt it. I was still too high on my post-sex bliss. His tongue brushed over the area, followed by a gentle kiss.

He rolled onto his back, tugging me with him. "Did I hurt you?"

"It was perfect."

His fingers brushed my hair aside so he could see me. His eyes fell to my neck. To his mark. "You're mine."

I pressed a kiss to his chest, just above his heart.

"I always was."

CHAPTER 21
PROWL

oc Paula waved us into her exam room.

"Lydia said you had an altercation with Rage yesterday."

Daff's shoulders stiffened.

"Lydia?"

"The on-call doctor who treated you," she answered, tugging a trolley to the side of the examination bed. "She moonlights between here and the lab. Who's first?"

"Knock-knock." The vet walked in, not waiting to be invited. "Did I miss anything?"

"You're right on time. Daff, do you want to go first?"

"Sure," she said, eyes flicking between the three of us.

I followed her over and lifted her up, my hands lingering on her hips. We'd been together three more times since I'd marked her, and it still wasn't enough.

She smiled up at me. "Thanks, big guy."

I stepped out of the way but refused to let go of her.

"No dizziness or nausea since we saw you yesterday?"

"Nope."

"Good."

She dropped the light from Daff's pupils and froze.

"Is that what I think it is?"

Daff shifted her weight, and I firmed my grip on her hip. Her worried eyes flew to mine.

"What is it?" Helliot asked, stepping closer.

"I marked her."

"Jesus Christ!"

Doc Paula cleared her throat. "Did you bite her anywhere else?"

"I marked her," I repeated. "Not mauled her."

"Only there, and only the once," Daff said, clarifying further.

Doc Paula didn't look relieved. "Have you had penetrative sex?"

"Of course they have!" Doctor Jerk-off sneered. "I've paged Lara and Jean. They're on their way."

Daff's teeth sank into her bottom lip, drawing a purr from me.

"Do you want me to check your ribs or shoulder again?"

"No, thank you," she whispered.

Doc Paula sighed. "I'll be blunt. We can't undo what's happened, but you need to be smart going forward, and unprotected sex isn't smart, hybrid or human. Are you on any birth control?"

"No."

"You need to be. If I don't have your preference on hand, I can order it in. But you'll need to abstain until you're covered, because we don't have the condom situation sorted yet, and although preliminary inquiries suggest the hybrids have a resistance to STIs it's not a theory we want to test."

"We're here," Lara said, entering the room with Jean hot on her heels. "What's happened?"

"The hybrid claimed her with a mating bite, and they've had unprotected sex."

Lara blinked a few times.

"Did you fully consent to both?" Jean asked.

The growl escaped before I could stop it. Daff grabbed my wrist, pulling it off her hip to squeeze between her trembling hands.

"Absolutely yes, to both."

Jerk-off snorted. "At this point, she'd say anything to protect him."

"How dare you!" she shot back, eyes spitting fire. "You want to know the truth? The truth is I begged him for it! For all of it! Every. Single. Time."

My cock twitched at the reminder of just how much she'd wanted me.

"Can I see the bite?" Lara asked, interrupting their line of sight.

Daff pulled the neck of her shirt aside, exposing the full length of her shoulder.

"Does it hurt?"

She licked her lips, looking nervous again. "Not much."

Doc Paula pulled open the top drawer of her trolley. "I'll give it a swab and get you an ointment that will help prevent scarring—"

"NO! I mean, no, thank you. I want to keep it."

Fuck, if that didn't fill my entire being with unbridled joy.

The Doc turned to Lara. "We'd just started discussing birth control and their need to abstain from sex until she's properly covered. We don't know how fertile Prowl is, and we aren't medically prepared for pregnancy or newborns needing medical intervention."

"What did you decide?" Jean asked.

"What are my choices?"

Something twisted in my stomach at her question. Was she asking to keep the peace? Or because she didn't want a family with me? She wanted to carry my mark. Did she not want to carry my cubs?

"If I don't have what you want on hand, I can order it in. The easiest to maintain coverage are IUDs and implants. But we can do injections or the oral pill if you prefer."

Daff nodded. "Can I think on it?"

Doc Paula pursed her lips. "I'll need to know by tomorrow morning."

"They need to be separated, not put on birth control!" Helliot snapped.

My heart thumped when no one jumped in to argue with him.

"No."

"It's not your choice," the vet sneered. "A mating bite clearly states a level of connection and dependency beyond healthy for your situation. You should have been separated the moment her calming your lion's instincts changed from clinical help to emotional connection."

"We can't undo what's happened," Jean said.

"No, but we can sure as hell start fixing it."

"What are you suggesting?" Lara asked him, meeting his angry gaze head-on.

"Exposure therapy, starting now. Six hours, twelve hours, eighteen hours, then twenty-four. Repeating the failed window of time as many times as necessary until Prowl can handle their permanent separation."

Daff's knuckles turned white from how hard she gripped my hand.

"Do you agree?" Lara asked the other female.

"It's a reasonable plan. If we don't intervene now..." She looked at Daff with a hint of pity. "Everyone here is on a contract, so there's only one way this can end. We must do what's best for Prowl's long-term health."

"Do we get a say in any of this?" she asked.

"No," Lara answered, her voice gentle but firm. "Paula's right. We need to do what's ultimately best for the hybrids' overall health and wellbeing."

Daff nodded, and I pulled her to me, my sweet Angel doing her best to blink back tears.

"Where will I go?"

"I've paged the care centre. Mandy's being relieved for the day; she'll be waiting for you at your apartment. I'll take you there as soon as the Doc Paula's finished with you."

"We're starting now?" I asked.

Jean met my gaze, his expression impressively blank. "Yes."

"There's nothing else I need from Daff. But I will need her to come back in the morning with her choice of contraception. I think it's the smart choice forward, whatever happens over the next few weeks."

She nodded against my chest.

I pressed a kiss to the top of her head. "I'll walk you out."

"It's best you don't. You'll only make it harder than it needs to be."

Lara's words felt like they bordered on betrayal. She was meant to stand up for us. For our health and wellbeing, and our happiness.

Daff was all those and more to me.

"And I still need to check your stitches," Doc Paula added.

Daff swallowed as I lifted her down, her damp eyes staring up at me.

"Six hours, Angel. We'll see each other again soon."

"Will you be okay?"

"Knowing you wear my mark and are coming back to me? Yes."

"Okay."

Then she was stepping away, following Jean out the exam room door.

CHAPTER 22
DAFF

Mandy was waiting for me, just like Jean said.

"What happened?" she asked, pulling me into a hug. "They said I was relieved for the day, because you needed me at our apartment."

"I'm sorry, I—"

"Holy shit! What happened to your neck?"

My hand shot to where I knew it showed, hovering over it, but not quite willing to cover it.

I didn't want to hide the mark that branded me his. "It's a mating bite."

"Right. In we go," she said, tugging my hand. "I've got chocolate stashed in my bedside table, and I have the feeling we'll be needing it by the end of whatever it is you're about to tell me."

She pointed to a dove grey, three-seater couch. "Sit. I'll be back in a moment."

When she did, I told her everything. The connection we felt. Him watching me, and me watching him. Coming together. How he begged to mark me, and I begged him to fuck me.

"Do you love him?"

"So freaking much."

"And you don't regret any of it, knowing you'll have to leave him at the end of your contract?"

I shrugged, so far past caring how I must look, all puffy and tear-stained.

"No one's ever loved him before. No one's held his hand or hugged him."

"Or fucked him."

I choked out a laugh. "That too."

"Was it good? Did it really feel like, you know..." she trailed off to boop the tip of her nose.

I fell back against the couch, clutching my almost empty box of tissues. "I'm trying to be serious!"

"You think I'm not?" she asked, waggling her eyebrows.

"Oh, my god," I said, shaking my head. "It was amazing," I finally said, all humour gone from my voice. "Everything about him... I don't think I could ever love someone else like I do him. So yeah, even though I know I'll leave, and it'll shatter me, heart and soul, to do it, loving him is absolutely worth it."

"Oh honey," she said, pulling another tissue out of the box in my hand and passing it to me. "So why all the tears now, when leaving is still so far away?"

"Because if this is what six hours of separation feels like, how will I cope when it's the rest of my life?"

"Would you stay if they let you?"

"So I could be with him? Yeah."

"You could really walk away from the rest of the world? From your Dad?"

"He'd be okay. My brothers are close by, and I'd send the money from here home. He'd have everything he needed, including a full-time carer if he wanted."

"And you'd have Prowl."

"And I'd have Prowl."

"What?" I asked, when she hadn't spoken for a few minutes.

"Did they make you take a Plan B pill?"

My heart thudded in my chest. "No."

"So, there's a chance..." she trailed off, looking at my stomach.

My hand moved on its own, settling on the space below my belly button. "They don't even know if it's possible."

"That doesn't mean it isn't."

"You're right."

"Would you keep it, if you were?"

Fire blazed through me, burning with the fierce need to protect the potential life within me.

"Yes."

"And Prowl?"

"I don't know. We haven't talked about it."

"That might be something you should do relatively soon. It might also prove a worthy enough reason to let you stay."

I closed my eyes, hope and fear clashing within me.

"Right," she said, jumping off the couch. "I'm getting popcorn. You choose the first movie. It's time to show you why I'm the best roommate ever."

Three movies, two bags of popcorn, and one much smaller emotional meltdown later, our six hours were up, and I was on my way back to Prowl.

He swooped me up into his arms when I entered, nuzzling his mating mark.

"You came back."

"You were worried I wouldn't?"

He shook his head. "Not by choice."

He let my body slide down the front of his until my feet hit the ground again.

"How did you go?"

"Fine," he said, tugging me towards our bed. "Knowing you wore my mark and no one could take it from you kept the beast in me calm."

"Did you stay here?"

"I was with King in his quarters. This place doesn't sit well with him, and I don't want to be here without you with me. How's Mandy?"

I sighed in contentment as I nudged his head onto my chest so I could run my fingers through his hair while we talked.

"Patient, thoughtful, and ridiculously sweet."

"I'm glad you have a friend here."

"Me too. I feel a little bad, though. I think she wanted to know more about what happened with Rage, but I was too upset about everything and worried about you and us, and what'll happen next to really talk about it."

"It's nice she cares about him."

"Hmmmm."

He took a deep breath, making the muscles on his back expand and contract. "Did you make your decision on birth control?"

"Do you want a family? Kids of your own?"

"Would you want them with me, knowing what they might look like?"

Tears pricked my eyes, but I kept my hand steady, grazing his scalp with my nails as I continued running my fingers through his hair.

"What if I'm already pregnant?"

He jerked up to look at me.

"They didn't make me take the morning-after pill, and as long as I don't, there's a chance…"

His lips met mine in a searing kiss before pulling away.

"Is it wrong to hope for it if it means I'll never have to leave you?"

He rolled us over, so I lay on top of him. "Don't take it."

Relief and a rush of happiness washed over me. "I won't."

"Don't take any of them."

"They won't like that."

"Fuck what they like."

I tilted my face up to look at him. "Doctor Helliot won't let this go. If it looks like we're fighting him on it, he'll push his agenda of separating us even harder."

"I don't want you taking it," he repeated, stroking my cheek. "I know it might not be possible, but I can't help but hope."

I sighed, snuggling back into him. "Me too."

"Then we'll hope together."

CHAPTER 23
DAFF

We were supposed to go back to medical. They were waiting on my choice of birth control, and Doctor Helliot would be wanting a debrief on how Prowl coped during our 'exposure therapy.'

I didn't want to deal with it, or anything else related to us spending time apart. By the way Prowl was holding me, neither did he.

So we figured we'd wait. Draw out our peaceful reverie with orgasm after orgasm until they demanded our presence. But the demand never came. Whether it was a miracle or because of someone else's disaster, their silence meant we spent the day in bed, learning each other's bodies like our lives depended on it.

Prowl kissed the top of my head. "They'll send in the guard if we don't answer it."

"Screw the phone. And the guard."

His chest moved beneath my cheek with his sigh, his fingers tracing lazy spirals over my lower back. "Except I'd have to kill anyone else who saw you like this, and that'd get me locked up or put down."

"Possessive much?"

"Yes."

I snorted. "I love how you don't even try to deny it."

"Why would I? You're mine."

I lifted my head just far enough to kiss his chest. "Always."

The phone on the wall started again, making me groan. His lips dove for mine, kissing me just long enough and deep enough to make my clit pulse. He slapped my ass through the sheet, flipped me over, then pecked my lips again before leaving me for the damn phone.

"Cheeky asshole."

He raised an eyebrow in my direction, letting me know he'd heard me.

"Yes? What time? We'll be there." He hung it back on its cradle but stayed a few seconds before turning around.

"When?"

"They're waiting for us now."

I stared up at the roof, trying my best to swallow the panic trying to claw its way up my throat.

"I don't want to go."

His face filled my vision, his sandy hair falling on either side of us, shielding us, this moment, from the rest of the waiting world.

"You're mine, Daff. I won't let them keep us apart."

"We won't be able to stop them. They could lock you up, send me back early—they could do so many things, Prowl, and we'd be helpless to stop them."

"Lara wouldn't allow it. She's on our side. All the hybrids are. And if push comes to shove, I'd bet Jean and a few of the women in your group would support us, too."

"What if Helliot goes above them? There are higher-ups that even Lara and Jean can't say no to."

"Then we'd stage a fucking revolt."

"We?"

"Hybrids. All of us. We won't let them take the hope of a partner, love, and a family from us. We're not willing to settle like we were. None of us are, not after seeing us together."

What else could I do but trust him? In him and us?

"Okay."

"We've got this, Angel. I promise. Now get that perfect ass up so we can get this over with."

I sighed but rolled said ass out of bed and hustled it out the door.

Doctor Helliot and Doc Paula were waiting for us. Because it was late afternoon, a few people were milling about in the waiting room. Their curious looks followed us past them and down the hall. We stopped outside an open office door.

"Daff first."

"No."

"What? Why?" I asked, looking between them.

Doctor Helliot crossed his arms. "Prowl's exposure therapy isn't just about time separation. It's about proving him capable of facing different situations and personal interactions that you'd usually do together."

"No," Prowl repeated.

I tugged on his beard, drawing his unhappy gaze.

"Remember what we spoke about last night?"

He scanned my face, thinking it over.

"I don't like it."

"I know. But we need to pick our battles. This isn't one of them."

He kissed the top of my head with a resigned sigh and stepped back.

Helliot watched, remaining until I followed Doc Paula inside. He shut the door behind us.

"What did you decide?" she asked, cutting to the chase.

"The pill, please."

"There are better options that—"

"I'm sure."

"What's your reasoning?" Helliot asked.

Dickwad. My contraception choice wasn't any of his business.

But Doc Paula looked interested in my answer. Which, in all honesty, was so I could flush the damn things down the toilet every morning.

Lucky I already had an alternative answer that was actually true.

"I can't handle the thought of a foreign object inside me that I can't remove on my own."

Helliot huffed, but Doc Paula nodded.

"And I don't want to be stuck feeling sick as a dog if I react badly to the injections. Once it's in my body, it's there till it dissipates. The pill is controllable and easily changed if it doesn't sit well with me."

"Okay," Doc Paula said, looking at Helliot. "Her reasons are reasonable, and she can start them today."

"Speaking of pills, did you take one yesterday?"

Rage scalded my insides.

"Excuse me?"

He waved in my general direction. "To get rid of anything that might have taken."

"Are you fucking with me right now?"

"No, Daphne. I'm one hundred percent serious."

"Lucus—"

"My body, my choice!"

"Not while you're under contract on my base!"

"Show me." He looked at Doc Paula, who'd rose to her feet.

"Show you what?"

"Where in her contract it states you, Lucus Helliot, can force her to take an abortive substance."

"I don't have to—"

"Yes, you do. Show me it right now, in clear, black and white letters, or drop the subject."

"Paula—"

"Her body, her choice, Lucus. That's not a topic that's up for debate."

He leaned back in his chair, fingers tapping the table as he stared at me.

"Consider it dropped. For now."

Thank god.

"My report on yesterday's separation stated Prowl coped without incident."

"Your report?"

"Which means it's time for your twelve-hour stint. You'll be doing that tonight."

"That's too soon!"

"The deal was advancement to the next time block, each time the previous one was a success. Nothing was said about the amount of time, or lack thereof, between them."

I looked to the woman who'd just spoken up for me.

"He's correct."

For a split, glorious second, I imagined myself picking up my chair and hurling it at him.

"When?"

"Before dinner."

"That's barely an hour away!"

"Enough time to collect your things and find somewhere else to sleep."

"Why are you forcing this? We have twenty-three months to build his capacity for this."

"What he feels for you isn't love, Daphne. He doesn't understand the concept."

"You don't know that."

"Gratitude, infatuation, lust, the yearning for emotional connection, and the intense desire to own something, when nothing, not even the clothes on his back, has ever belonged to him," he said, ticking off his fingers. "That is what he feels for you.

"You having feelings for him will only hurt you. To him, you are replaceable. He might not think so now, but he will. Once his lust is sated, the excitement has worn off, and he realises you're not the only one with a pair of tits and willing—"

"Enough, Lucus, you've made your point."

"Fuck. You. What have you done for him, for any of them, except shred the remnants of their non-existent self-worth, and the belief that anyone could ever love, want or accept them, exactly as they are!

"I'll gladly walk away from here, shattered into a million unfixable pieces, if it means leaving with him finally understanding his true worth as a person. His worth in my eyes, not yours."

"We'll see if he agrees with you once he realises he doesn't need you anymore."

Doc Paula cleared her throat. "I think that's enough for now. If you're happy to wait in the room next door, we'll touch base with Prowl, and I'll fetch you your pills.

"Usually, we'd wait until the first day of your next cycle, but I recommend starting them now, and not engaging in penetrative sex for the next two weeks."

She opened the door for me.

"I'll see you tomorrow, Daphne," Helliot said to my already turned back.

"My name's not Daphne, asshole."

Prowl was standing at the other end of the corridor, talking with another hybrid. He must've been watching the door because he was striding towards me the moment I stepped out.

"Are you alright?"

I closed my eyes, trying to calm the storm raging inside me. It would only make things worse if he realised how upset I really was, right before he went in and got news of our imminent separation.

"Fine. Doc Paula's putting me next door while I wait."

The backs of his fingers brushed my cheek.

"I won't be long."

I forced a smile for him. "Okay."

Paula showed me into her office.

"Make yourself comfortable."

"Thanks."

She hovered by the door. "We'll be next door if you need us."

Yeah, I'd be happy placing a decent size bet on that not being what she'd wanted to say.

Time dragged. The lack of growls, screams and roaring was comforting, but it was driving me nuts that I couldn't hear what they were saying.

I shot to my feet when I heard their door open, and Doc Paula telling Prowl she'd be back in a minute. Then he was filling my doorway; jaw clenched, hands flexing in and out of fists by his sides.

"You know?"

"Yeah."

"They don't want me going back with you. They're going to take me straight over to King's."

"Are you okay with that?"

"Do I have a choice?"

My hand slid up his forearm, trying to soothe his tense muscles.

"I'm impressed you kept your shit together when they told you."

"Someone told me to pick my battles."

"I hate being away from you."

He tugged me towards him, wrapping both arms around me. "Me too, Angel. At least you'll get to sleep through most of it."

More like I'd binge-watch something until I either passed out or Helliot's twelve-hour timer ran out.

"You should try to sleep too."

"Without your scent in my lungs?"

I smiled up at him. "I love you, Prowl."

"Fuck," he whispered, squishing me to him. "I love you too, Angel. So damn much."

"If you two are done?" Doc Paula asked from behind Prowl.

He stepped to my side so we were both facing her.

"Your pills," she said, handing them over. "Try to take them at the same time every night, starting today. And no sex for two weeks, since there's no condoms and you should never trust the pull-out method."

"Thanks," I said, feeling Prowl's eyes on me as I took the box.

"There's a cart outside waiting for you. It'll run you up to collect your things, then drop you off at your apartment. Prowl, King's not far behind."

"Can I walk her out?"

Her eyes flicked to Doctor Asshole's door. "Better not."

He stopped a hairsbreadth from my lips. "I'll see you tomorrow."

I lifted onto my toes, closing the tiny space between us to kiss him. "Be safe. And try to sleep. It'll help the time go quicker."

I felt his eyes on me, watching me walk away from him.

Pete, one of the officers who rotated door duty for Prowl's enclosure, waved to me.

"You're my taxi driver?"

"Yes, Mam."

"What a thrilling job you have."

He chuckled at my dry tone. "Not so much these days, but that's not a bad thing."

That piqued my interest. "How long have you been here?"

"Since the hybrids moved in."

Huh.

"How long's your contract?"

"Three years."

"It doesn't bother you, going so long without leaving?"

He shrugged. "The money's good, the job's unique, and there's no one waiting at home for me."

"Do you think they'll offer you another contract?"

Did they do that for the military-trained personnel here?

"I was told I could extend it for as long as I like."

"Wait, really?"

"Don't look so excited," he said, glancing at me. "I'm male, an officer, and not at risk of becoming emotionally involved with a hybrid."

"How do they know?"

"Excuse me?"

"How do they know you won't get emotionally involved with a hybrid?"

"I don't swing that way."

"Some people would die for their best friend."

He shook his head, either not willing or not wanting to comment. "I'll wait here while you get your things."

I was in and out in two minutes. Pillow, toothbrush, and comfy clothes I could wallow in. The closer we got to Mandy's apartment—I couldn't seem to accept that it was mine too—my list of things I should have grabbed had grown exponentially longer.

Brush. Deodorant. Socks. Underwear. Toothpaste.

There were only so many things I could reasonably ask to borrow from Mandy.

The apartment was empty when I got there. My thumb unlocked the door, which was unnerving since I wasn't sure when or how they would have got my print, and the note on the kitchen counter said she'd be back in fifteen.

She was picking up dinner from the eatery, so we didn't have to socialise or cook.

I walked through the apartment, looking through the kitchen cabinets, checking how big the shower was, and at the end of the short hall, found the room that was supposed to be mine.

I tossed my things onto the bed, a double with plain white sheets, and flopped onto my back next to them. It felt... empty. And the furthest thing from mine.

But if things kept going the way Doctor Helliot wanted, this room would end up mine a hell of a lot sooner than I wanted.

Would Prowl end up back in the hybrid residential area, living with King? Or did they get their own places? I couldn't see him claiming a home in the Wild Zone like Rage, but if he ended up feeling like Doctor Helliot said, not actually loving or wanting me, once the shine wore off and he realised he didn't need me anymore, then maybe he would?

I shook my head, refusing to let his words poison my thoughts.

Prowl loved me. I was sure of it. Our connection was real.

It wouldn't disappear just because he didn't need me anymore.

I was sure of it.

CHAPTER 24
PROWL

Daff wasn't here.

The waiting room was empty and held no trace of her scent.

Doctor Asshole exited the corridor to my left, eyes running over me.

"You survived."

Because King had sat against his door all night, watching me stalk the room like a caged cat.

"Barely."

"Barely is still an acceptable result. Follow me."

He walked off, assuming I would follow.

"Where's Daff?"

He sat behind his desk, looking like he had all the time in the world, while my lion raged within, desperate to see her.

"Close the door."

"Where is she?"

"Delayed," he said, when I refused to move. "If you want more answers, you'll close the door."

Was this a battle I wanted to fight?

Abso-fucking-loutely.

Would I?

No. Because Daff was my end game, and I was desperate to see her. Which meant getting through this shit show as fast as possible.

"How do you feel you went?"

"Fine."

"No flashbacks, mood swings, bouts of rage, no violence towards property, yourself, or others?"

"No."

"Successful, then."

I grunted.

It hadn't felt successful. More like a slow, painful death that was only survivable because I knew she was safe, hopefully happy, and wearing my mark.

"You need to seriously consider your next course of action."

"Trialling eighteen hours of separation?" I asked. Because of course the asshole would be pushing for the next one already.

"That's one of them."

The only other course of action I was interested in was putting an end to this farce, and him leaving Daff and I the hell alone.

"You have other options."

I impressed myself by not rolling my eyes. "You've made it perfectly clear I don't."

"You do have options. They just haven't been ones you're interested in hearing."

"Your options aren't in my best interest."

"But what if they're in Daff's?"

"What are you saying?"

"I'm not saying anything. I'm asking you to look past

your own inclinations and think about what's best for her. You've spent your life in one cell or another. This," he said, waving about the room, "Is paradise to you. But what is it for her? Here, you are free, but she'll always be trapped.

"She'll never buy her dream home. Study the degree she always wanted. Find a partner who can wine and dine and travel the world with her. She'll never kiss her kids goodbye on their first day of school. She might never be a Mother, depending on your fertility.

"Then there's the family she has that she'll never see again. Her Father, her brothers. Nieces. No Christmas gatherings, Easter egg hunts, trick or treating with her family, current or future.

"No romantic weekend getaways, Father's Day dinners, introducing her partner to her family and friends. Or just never speaking to any of them again. Is that really the life you want for her?"

Fuck.

"She's mine."

"Yes, and she's made it clear she returns the sentiment. And willing to fight for whatever it is you both think you have together. So it's up to you to do the right thing. For her."

A growl lodged in my throat, fighting for freedom. "The right thing would be letting us stay together."

"For you, maybe. But for her?"

He let his question hang between us.

"The longer this continues, the harder it will be on her when she leaves. You'll have the support of everyone here. People with shared memories who can comfort and reminisce with you. But Daff? Her NDA means she can't breathe a word about you or your relationship with anyone.

"Her heartbreak will be hers alone and borne in silence,

with no way to share or unburden herself. Not to family, friends or even a therapist with the skills to help her.

"Is that what you want for her? Because that's what will happen if you don't end this now and give her time to heal here, with people she can actually talk to."

My head was raging. My heart was aching. My gut sinking with guilt.

Could I knowingly, willingly, take all those experiences from her? Or make her face the fallout of going back and hurting all on her own?

But there was one last stubborn piece of me resisting.

"If she's pregnant, none of it will matter."

He tapped his desk with the end of his pen. "For argument's sake, let's say you're fertile. And then, lucky enough again, to conceive a child by accident, with no concept of diet, supplements or tracking her cycles, from your initial rounds of unprotected sex.

"Let's say you managed to line that all up and didn't miscarry during the first trimester when risks are their highest with normal, healthy, human sperm. Or develop any number of inconceivable, fatal defects at any stage of the infant's gestation, as a result of your own mutated genetics. How likely do you truly think that pregnancy is?"

How could words spilled from this asshole's lips hurt more than any attempt to teach, train or control me ever had?

He tossed his pen onto his desk.

"Look, if a miracle happens, and she is, then we come at this from a different angle and do what we need to do. But for now, while that isn't the case, the sooner we act, the better. The longer this continues, the harder it will be for her."

I scrubbed my face with my hands, torn between destroying his office and puking my guts up.

He was asking me to do the impossible.

To give her up.

Not because I wanted to, but because it was the right thing for her.

She deserved more than me and this base. We weren't worth the sacrifices she'd make, the grief she'd carry.

Her coming into my life was already a miracle, more than I'd ever hoped for.

I dropped my hands, defeat choking me.

She didn't need to be with me to still be mine. I'd carry her in my heart and soul until the day I died.

However soon that ended up being.

"Reassign me to the Wild Zone. I'll settle near Rage. If I reach the point of needing another cell, put me down."

"You'll need to sign off on your wishes while you're clear-headed."

I nodded.

He pulled open the bottom drawer of a filing cabinet, skimming through the tabs and pulling out a file. He flipped it open, revealing a picture of me, at the time of my rescue, and half a dozen other pages of notes.

He pushed one towards me.

"Sign that. Both sides."

The pen felt like it weighed half a ton in my hand, hovering as I skimmed over the document.

And signed on the dotted line. Twice.

He added his signature beside them.

"I'll see the appropriate people know about your decision. You're doing the right thing," he said, returning the folder and closing the draw.

And that's all that mattered. Doing the right thing for Daff, for her long term happiness.

"I'll go there now."

I couldn't handle seeing her. One look, one whiff, and I'd grab hold of her and refuse to let go.

"Someone will collect your personal items and leave them at the gate."

I nodded.

What else was there to say?

CHAPTER 25
DAFF

"Did they say why?" I looked up from my bouncing knee.

"No. Just the time change. Do you think something happened last night?"

"They'd want you with him sooner, not later, if it had."

"Do you think..." Nope. Nope. Nope. I refused to go there.

She sat beside me, the smell of her morning coffee twisting my stomach. "Do I think what?"

Damn it.

"Do you think he's avoiding me? Putting off seeing me."

"Are you serious right now?"

I shrugged. "He made it through the night. If he's realised he doesn't need me anymore..."

"What the hell, Daff!"

I shook my head. "Right. Sorry. I'm being crazy. I am being crazy, right?"

"Yes. You are. He loves you, Daff. His entire world revolves around you."

I closed my eyes, my fingers finding his mark on my shoulder.

"I know. I just...something doesn't feel right."

She squeezed my knee. "Everything will be fine. And if it's not, we'll figure out how to fix it."

In an ideal world, yes. But this was a government-owned base, Prowl's existence was a well-kept secret, and I was on a contract they could terminate any time they wanted.

If something was wrong, I had zero power to change it.

"Do you want me to come with you? I've got time."

"No. Thank you."

"Are you walking, or are they sending a cart?"

"Golf cart."

"If you change your mind, I—"

Knocking cut her off.

"That's them." I rubbed my palms down the front of my thighs before hugging her.

"Thank you for trying to keep me sane."

"Thank you for letting me eat most of the ice cream."

I snorted. "Don't get used to it."

"Good luck."

"Thanks, Mandy."

Another squeeze, and she let me go.

The drive was quiet. The waiting room decently busy for nine am. And it took fifteen minutes before Doctor Helliot appeared from the same hallway as yesterday.

"Daff."

Was Prowl already in his office, waiting for me? I hurried after him but froze in his doorway.

There was no one else here.

"Where's Prowl? And Doc Paula?"

"Paula's not needed, and Prowl's already been here."

My stomach fell to my toes. "Is he coming back?"

"No."

I pressed a hand to my chest, where I could feel a physical ache threatening to split me open.

"Where is he?"

"He's relocated to the Wild Zone."

"What? No. He wouldn't do that."

He pushed a piece of paper towards me.

I glanced down at it. "What am I looking at?"

"His relocation request. And on the other side, his kill order. He's decided to be put down instead of captured, contained or isolated if the need should arise again."

"No," I repeated, picking it up so I could read it for myself.

"That's his signature on the bottom, on both sides."

I shoved it back at him.

"You did this."

"I had nothing to do with his decision."

"I don't believe you!"

"You don't need to. His signature is all that matters, and he gave it twice."

"He loves me."

"He's left you the only way he can."

My hand dropped to my lower stomach. His eyes caught the movement.

"Trapping him with a child won't work. The hybrids weren't raised with morals or ideals. As far as he's concerned, you're in his past, and a child, if there is one, is no longer his problem to deal with."

God, that hurt hearing. But it also sounded nothing like him.

I'd rocked his world when I said I wouldn't take that damn pill, and he'd responded by demanding I not take any of them. He wanted a family with me just as much as I did with him.

He may have signed those papers, but I didn't believe for a moment it was because he didn't want me anymore.

He was mine, and I was his, and I was going to do whatever the hell I needed to make sure he knew it.

I needed a plan.

~

"Hey," Mandy said, pausing in the doorway. Her eyes darted around her lounge room, looking for someone who wasn't there. "I wasn't expecting to see you."

"We have a problem."

"Another round of exposure therapy?"

"No. A real problem. He moved himself to the Wild Zone and signed off on a kill order."

"What does that mean?"

"It means that if he loses all his progress and is faced with being locked inside another room, he wants to be put down instead."

"He can tell them to do that?"

"If he signs off on it while clear-headed."

She ditched her bag on the coffee table. "Do you know why?"

I flopped back on the couch.

"Why did he ask to move to the Wild Zone when the last time I saw him, he was kissing the mark he left on me and telling me he loved me? Why else? He's an idiot!"

"Okay... but more specifically?"

"My guess? He thinks he's doing what's best for me. That if I'm not pregnant, I'll have to leave at the end of my contract, broken-hearted and unable to tell anyone, so he'd rather rip the Band-Aid off now, and I'll either hate him for abandoning me or give up on him completely, and return to the outside world fine and dandy."

"I see what you mean by idiot."

"Right!"

"But -"

I shot daggers at her with my eyes, a glare that would have made lesser men crumble.

"Hear me out."

"Ugh. I'm listening."

"What if he's right? What if it is, as heartbreaking as it feels, better to end things now, before you're in too deep?"

"I'm already in too deep."

"Daff..."

"I'd rather have two years of love than a lifetime of regret. And I would regret it. I'd regret every missed moment of joy. Every night, we should have fallen asleep together, every kiss we would have shared, and the reasons behind them. I might face a lifetime of heartache, but I'd do it with a soul full of cherished memories."

"What do you need me to do?"

"You'll help me?"

"Hell yes. Let's find your lion and bring him back."

"I need to see him. A message or letter won't work. I need to do it in person."

"That means going into the Wild Zone."

"Yes," I said, sitting up straighter. "The gate is manned by wolves, so that should make getting in easier. But there's no way in hell they'd let me through on my own."

"Is there another hybrid you trust?"

"King will know where he is, but..."

"But?"

"But I don't know if he'll take me. He might think Prowl's better off where he is, and better off without me."

"There's only one way to find out."

"What are you doing?"

She was halfway to the kitchen, heading for the corded phone on the wall.

"I'm finding out whose side he's on. Yes? I need a

message put through to King's pager. It's Mandy. I work at the care centre with the cubs. Thank you. Call Mandy. 911. Apartment twenty-six. Great. Thank you."

She hung up the phone.

"What did you do?"

"Sent him a direct page, telling him to patch his call through to here."

"Why mention the cubs?"

"If I had his number, I could message him myself because I don't. I need admin to do it, and they always require a reason before sending it through."

"You lied to them!"

"No. I told them who I was and where I worked. And the message said to contact me ASAP. I didn't lie about anything."

She grinned, right as the phone started ringing.

"Hello? Yes, it's Mandy. The cubs are fine. This is about Daff."

I was half tempted to elbow my way in, so I could hear what he was saying.

"She's not okay with it and wants him to come back. Uh-huh. She doesn't care." She sent me a wink. "She said, and I quote, she'd rather 'two years of love than a lifetime of regret.' Okay. Thanks."

She hung it back on the wall.

"Do you want the good news, or the bad news?"

"Bad news."

She winced. "King might be slightly pissed at me for making him worry about the cubs. I'm not to use 911 with him again without stating who it's referring to."

My breath caught in my throat. "And the good news?"

"He'll meet you at the dining hall at 7 a.m. and take you to see him."

"Holy shit, you did it!" I squealed, bowling her over with a hug.

She squeezed me back. "I got the front door open. The rest is on you."

I pulled back to look at her. "You're the best friend I've ever had. I know that's not saying much, considering I could count them all on one hand with a few fingers left over, but I couldn't have asked for a better one."

"Believe it or not, I haven't had a whole lot myself."

Which was mind-blowing. How could anyone NOT be friends with this woman?

"I owe you big time."

She snorted. "Don't you forget it. I have every intention of collecting on it."

CHAPTER 26
DAFF

"Thank you."

King glanced at me. "He shouldn't have left."

"Tell him that."

"I plan to."

I grinned at him, despite my nerves wreaking havoc on my insides.

"I wasn't sure if you'd be for or against this."

"Why?"

I shrugged as I faced forward, ignoring the admin building passing on our left. No one in there knew what we were doing or where we were headed, but it still felt as if one look at me would reveal our intent, and my whole plan of going in there and demanding he come back out and be with me would be shot to hell.

"My last trip in didn't go so well."

"That wasn't your fault. He doesn't have a problem with you."

"Are we talking about the same incident? Cause I was only involved in one, and him knocking me down like a tank on steroids suggests it was, and he does."

He looked at me again. "It's not my place to say what

happened, other than it wasn't personal, and it wasn't you he was reacting to. If anything, he approves of you. And happy for Prowl."

"Okay."

"Okay? Just like that?"

"He wouldn't be in the Wild Zone if he didn't have issues. You and Prowl know him best, so if you think his reaction was because of his issues and not me as a person or as Prowl's, then I believe you."

"I appreciate that."

"And I appreciate you getting me inside the Wild Zone again."

"It won't be a problem unless Tracker's on shift."

"Why Tracker?"

"If he smells dishonesty, he won't let us through."

"And after what happened last time, the chances of me getting Jean's stamp of approval would be zero to none."

We were crossing the helipad now, the full length of the Wild Zone filling the horizon.

King let out a hiss long before I could see who was manning the gate.

"Tracker?"

"Yes."

"What do we do?"

"Watch our words and pray he's having a good day."

I could do that.

We ditched the golf cart, and I hustled my butt to keep up with him.

Tracker's face was leaner than the lion's, emphasising the way his jaw lengthened into an almost muzzle. He stood as tall as King, but only half as wide. Anyone else with those dimensions would look bean pole scrawny, but you could see his body was nothing but chorded muscle built for speed.

"King." His blue eyes slid over to me. "Daff."

"Hi, Tracker."

He folded his arms. "What can I do for you both?"

"Daff needs to see Prowl."

The wolf nodded. "I saw his relocation notice."

"Can we go in?"

"Do you know where you're going?"

"Finding him won't be an issue."

"It will be with her by your side. There's more than a few in there curious about her."

"Because of her last visit or word spreading about their relationship?" King asked.

"Both. Especially now that her suggestions got green-lighted."

I perked up at the news. "They did? Which ones?"

"All of them."

I looked at King. "If he doesn't get his ass out of there and into the shared living zone with me, there'll be hell to pay."

"He won't need much convincing."

"Better not," I huffed.

"He's with Rage," Tracker said, holding out a Taser.

"Thank you." I hoped he could hear how much I meant it.

"No incidents this time. I don't want to have to explain why I let you in."

"You got it. Or King's got it. Since he's responsible for me."

"Just until I get you to Prowl."

I grinned at him. "Just until you get me to Prowl."

I could handle the rest from there.

CHAPTER 27
PROWL

I rinsed the last plate and set it on the dish rack.

A growl followed.

"If you don't like how I stack it, do it yourself," I said, ignoring Rage's foul mood.

"Why are you still here?"

"Because I need a place to stay."

"The fuck you do. Find your own house."

"We've shared less space than this."

"Not by choice."

I tossed the wet dish towel on Rage's bench instead of hanging it. Did I know it would piss him off? Maybe. Did he deserve it? Yes. Yes, he did.

"You didn't say one word to me yesterday. What changed?"

Rage tilted his head to both sides, cracking his neck. "You shacking up here instead of pissing off."

"I told you I moved here."

"I didn't know you meant *my* house!"

"Go back to grunting at me."

"I will once you get the hell out."

"It's a few days, asshole."

He grunted.

Great. Back to that again.

"Where will you go?"

"When?" I asked, deciding to wipe down his sink.

"When you leave my house."

"Sarge said there's an unclaimed cabin to the west of you. He just needs to dot some Is and cross some Ts."

"Panthers are there."

"The cabin?"

"The area. Wouldn't take your woman there."

"She won't be coming this side of the fence."

Another grunt. "Sorry."

"For trying to kill her?"

He rubbed his face, his stance loosening for the first time since I arrived.

He'd been less than impressed to find me on his doorstep before he'd even had the chance to do his morning shit.

"I'm protective of my home. I wasn't prepared for her coming inside. I didn't think. I just needed to stop her."

"So me being here..."

"Is a pain in my ass."

"Noted."

"She seems nice."

"Did you gather that from your vast experience with women or the thirty seconds of looking at her before almost killing her?"

"You called her yours, asshole! She'd have to be nice to put up with you."

"I marked her."

He stilled, eyes going wide.

"And there's a chance she's pregnant. If that's possible for us."

"Then what the fuck are you doing here!"

I walked past him, ignoring the question, only to jerk to a stop thanks to the iron grip on my arm.

"I said, what, the fuck, are you doing here?"

"I ended it."

"Does she love you? Despite what we are?"

"Yes."

"You wouldn't have marked her if you didn't feel the same way."

"Your point?"

"What brand of insanity would make you give up a single second of your time with her?"

"She can't stay."

"So? Follow her home."

"Right. I'll just book my seat on the chopper next to her. That'd go down real well."

"Then climb the damn cliff, jump off and swim to her!"

"I can see the headlines now. Human/animal mutation shot dead on the beach."

He didn't just let go of my arm; he shoved me backwards with it.

"You don't deserve her. Let one of the other hybrids have her. There's no way in hell they'd quit on her."

"She's mine!"

"I don't see you with her!"

"She wears my mark!"

"You think any of them will give two shits about your teeth having been in her when she's warming their bed every night?"

"Shut the fuck up!"

"No!"

I needed to get out of here. The walls were too close, and there wasn't enough air. I could barely catch my breath.

The bastard followed me outside.

"Would you trade a single one of your memories with her?"

I bent over, my hands on my knees, as I focused on breathing.

"No. Not for anything."

"You wouldn't trade the peace of never knowing her for the pain of loving and losing her?"

"No, Rage! What's your fucking point?"

"My point, dumbass, is she probably feels the same way. And instead of asking her which option she'd prefer, you've made the choice for her, abandoning her and wasting god knows how many months of extra memories you could have made together!"

Shit. It was getting harder to breathe, not easier.

"I fucked up."

"No shit."

I fell back on my ass, putting my head between my knees.

"What's wrong with you?"

"Can't breathe."

"Calm the fuck down. You'll be fine."

"Asshole."

"Incoming."

Could I not catch a damn break?

"I'm going inside."

"Wait!"

"They're not here for me, and I don't want a repeat of last time."

"What?" Breathe damn it! "Rage!"

"Prowl?"

Yep. I was well on my way to passing out, and the bastard had left me here, on my own, with someone heading towards me.

"Prowl!"

I looked up to see her bolting towards me, King keeping pace beside her. Then she was in front of me, her face filling my vision, her scent filling my lungs.

"Angel?"

"What's wrong?" she asked, her small hands fluttering over me. "What happened? Are you hurt?"

"I'm sorry," I managed, grabbing hold of her wrists. "I fucked up."

"King? He's struggling to breathe! Help him!"

"He's having a panic attack."

She froze, looking at him like he'd lost his mind. "He's what?"

"Panic attack," I repeated, pulling her onto my lap. "Just need to hold you."

She melted into me like I hadn't tried my best to shatter our world yesterday morning.

"I'm sorry."

"I know."

I took a deeper breath, the smell of her hair easing the passage of air into my lungs. "I shouldn't have walked away."

"No, you shouldn't have."

"I thought I was doing the right thing for you."

She patted my chest like she was humouring me. "I know."

"Do you forgive me?"

"As long as you move back out of here and undo your termination order for as long as I'm here."

"Done."

She patted my chest again. "Is it wrong to feel satisfied that Helliot's going to shit bricks over this?"

I kissed the top of her head, pulling her closer. "No. But we still have a timer hanging over our heads. And he'll keep trying to separate us."

"So, we'll play it smart. Spend our days together, sleep in

our allocated apartments, and push like hell to have the first available place in the shared living area."

"If they approve one."

"They have," King said from somewhere to my left. "Not sure how long it will take to happen, but Tracker said it got the green light. All of Daff's suggestions did."

I squeezed her. "Will you be okay if we do this, and you still have to leave at the end of your contract?"

"We have twenty-three months to keep pushing for change. If others form relationships, they'll join the push, too. It's not over 'til it's over, and I'd rather go out fighting, loving you so much my heart hurts, than pretending you don't mean the world to me, and leave here with a lifetime of regret."

My hand found her jaw, tilting her perfect face up to mine.

"I love you so damn much, Angel. You walking into my life changed everything."

She met my kiss halfway, gripping me in a way that spoke to my soul.

Because of her, I'd found my home.

My peace.

My family.

And gave us all a reason to hope.

EPILOGUE - DAFF

T hree Weeks Later.

PROWL LOOKED at me in alarm. "What happened? Do you need a doctor?"

I pushed at his chest, stopping his frantic search of my body. "You can... smell it?"

"You're bleeding."

I swallowed, nodding. "Yeah. I got my period."

I didn't have the most regular cycles, and we had a lot going against us, but I'd still hoped.

"It's okay, Angel," he whispered, wiping my tears with his thumb. "He said our chances were small."

"He?"

"Doctor jerk-off."

I snorted a laugh, despite my aching heart. "I hate he was right."

"Me too," I whispered, letting him pull me into a hug. "Me staying will be harder now."

He kissed the top of my head. "We were always going to need to fight for it. We just have more motivation now."

"I want to ask you something, but I'm worried it's too selfish of me."

He gripped the back of my neck, his eyes flicking between mine. "Anything."

"Can you be the first volunteer?"

"For the fertility testing?"

"Yeah," I whispered, wiping another tear. "I don't think I can handle feeling like this every cycle, only to find out it's never been possible. I feel awful asking. I know how you all feel about tests—"

"I'll do it."

"You will?"

"If it spares you this? Yes."

I lifted onto my toes, pulling him down for a kiss. "Thank you."

"Do you want to take your birth control pills until we know the answer?"

"Is that okay?"

"Whatever you need."

"Are you upset with me?"

"Why would I be upset? This isn't your fault, and I don't want you feeling like this if you don't have to." The immediate frown on his face backed up his words. But it stayed instead of melting away.

"Please talk to me," I whispered, reaching up to touch his jaw. "I need you to be honest with me about this. This kind of thing can break people, and I love you too much to risk us because we didn't want to hurt each other with how we're feeling."

He sighed. "I'm worried you'll choose to leave if I can't give you a family."

"That's not gonna happen, big guy. I won't lie and say it's

not what I want, because I want everything with you. But the most important part of that picture is you.

"If it can only be the two of us, then that's what it'll be. A part of me will be sad, but it'll never be more than the happiness of us being together."

He pressed his forehead to mine. "I love you so damn much."

"I love you too, Prowl."

The door alert sounded.

"Ugh. If I never hear that sound again, it'll be too soon."

He gave my forehead another kiss and stepped aside, looking at the guard who'd entered.

"Lara needs you," he said, looking at Prowl. "King's taken an unwilling female into the Wild Zone and is keeping her hostage."

"What?"

"How do you know she's unwilling?" Prowl asked.

"It's Kara."

He grabbed my hand, already moving for the door.

"There's a cart outside. They'll fill you in on the drive."

"Thanks," he called over his shoulder.

"What the hell happened to make King abduct someone? And Kara, of all people!"

Prowl shook his head. "I don't know. But we're about to find out."

AUTHOR NOTE

From the very bottom of my heart - Thank you.

YOU are amazeballs. For taking a chance on Prowl, and me, a brand spanking new Indie Author.

If you haven't heard, Prowl is the first in a fifteen book saga called the Spliced Love Series. OMG, right? I'm not sure if I'm laughing or crying about it, but once the hybrid idea hit, I realised there was going to be a *LOT* of males needing a happy ending (Literally and figuratively 😅)

Each book will focus on a new couple, and a solid HEA in every book from King onwards, and the full storyline following the developing rights of the hybrids (including compound attacks/world revelation/covert jobs requiring some hybrids to 'mask up' - there's some serious action coming) will be revealed throughout the series.

I'll be doing my best to release 3-4 books a year in this series, so you won't be waiting forever for the full line up.

King is next, followed by his companion book Night. As for Rage and Mandy, their story is book 4.

Finally, If you loved Prowl as much as I do, please leave him a review or a shout out on social media. Indie Authors thrive and survive on those stars and tags, so they are always incredibly appreciated.

Feel free to tag me - @natalie.starkoss on Insta & @natalie_starkoss on Tiktok, or visit my website (nataliestarkoss.com)

I can't wait for you to meet the rest of my hybrids and their mates! Until then, keep safe, and happy reading.

xx Nat

ABOUT NATALIE

Natalie Starkoss (She/Her) is an Australian (hello from Tasmania!) Indie Author writing Spicy Human/Other Romance. She's a sucker for HEA's, big size differences and MMC's who'd do anything for their female.

Things to know: She's a self proclaimed caffeine addict (Tea over coffee) loves reading Alien & Monster smut, her shadow is in the shape of a mini dachshund named Pippa, and if she's ever forced to choose, doughnuts over chocolate (not that eating chocolate is ever a hardship!)

Pop onto her website to see both her available and upcoming books, and the Author events she's attending.

You can also reach her through email - nat@nataliestarkoss.com